Maigret and the Pickpocket

Also available in Large Print
by Georges Simenon:

Maigret and the Headless Corpse
Maigret and the Toy Village

Maigret and the Pickpocket

Georges Simenon

Translated from the
French by Nigel Ryan

G.K. HALL & CO.
Boston, Massachusetts
1990

Published in Large Print by arrangement with
Harcourt Brace Jovanovich, Publishers.

G.K. Hall Large Print Book Series.

Set in 16 pt. Plantin.

Library of Congress Cataloging in Publication Data

Simenon, Georges, 1903–
    [Voleur de Maigret.   English]
    Maigret and the pickpocket / Georges Simenon : translated from
the French by Nigel Ryan.
        p.   cm.—(G.K. Hall large print book series)   (Nightingale
series)
    Translation of: Voleur de Maigret.
    ISBN 0-8161-4666-7 (lg. print)
    1. Large type books.   I. Title.
[PQ2637.I53V5713   1990]
843′.912—dc20
                                                                89-26794

Maigret and the Pickpocket

ONE

"SORRY . . ."

"Don't mention it . . ."

It was at least the third time, since the corner of Boulevard Richard-Lenoir, that in lurching she had thrust her bony shoulder into him and pressed her string shopping bag against his thigh.

She mumbled her excuses, neither embarrassed nor apologetic, after which she resumed staring straight ahead, with a settled and resolute air.

Maigret did not bear her any ill will. Anyone might have thought he found it entertaining to be jostled. He was in a mood to take everything lightly that morning.

He had chanced to see a bus with an open platform coming, which was already a source of satisfaction. This kind of transportation was becoming more and more rare, as such buses were being drawn from circulation; soon he would be obliged to empty out his pipe before being swallowed up inside one of these enormous modern conveyances in which the passenger feels like a prisoner.

There were the same open-platform buses when he had arrived in Paris nearly forty years before, and in those early days he never tired of riding up and down the main boulevards on the Madeleine-Bastille line. It had been one of his first discoveries.

And the café terraces. He never grew tired of the café terraces either, from which he could survey the ever changing street scene over a glass of beer.

Yet another marvel, that first year: you could go out of doors, from the end of February, without an overcoat. Not always, but occasionally. And the blossom was starting to come out along some of the avenues, in particular Boulevard Saint-Germain.

These memories were coming back to him, bit by bit, because this year once again spring had come early, and that morning he had left home without a coat.

He felt a lightness about himself, like the sparkle in the air. The colors of the shops, the groceries, the women's dresses, were gay and lively.

He was not really thinking. Only scraps of thoughts which didn't add up to a coherent whole. His wife would be taking her third driving lesson at ten o'clock that morning.

It was funny, unexpected. He couldn't have said exactly how it had been decided. When Maigret had been a young clerk, there was no question of affording a car. At the time it was unthinkable. And later on, he had never seen the need for one. It was too late for him to learn to drive. Too many other thoughts were always passing through his head. He wouldn't see the red lights, or else he would mistake the brake for the accelerator.

But it would be pleasant to drive to their cottage, at Meung-sur-Loire, on Sundays. . . .

They had just made up their minds, all of a sudden. His wife had protested, laughing.

"Just imagine . . . Learning to drive, at my age . . ."

"I'm sure you'll do very well . . ."

She was having her third lesson and was every bit as nervous as a young girl studying for her exams.

"How did it go?"

"The instructor is very patient."

His fellow passenger in the bus couldn't have been a car driver. Why had she come to do her shopping in the Boulevard Voltaire neighborhood, when she lived in another part of town? It was one of those little mysteries that tend to fasten themselves in one's mind. She was wearing a hat, an increasingly rare spectacle, especially in the morning. There was a chicken in her shopping bag, butter, eggs, leeks and celery. . . .

The harder object, at the bottom, which pressed into his thigh at every jolt, must be the potatoes. . . .

Why take the bus to buy perfectly ordinary provisions miles away from home, when they were readily available anywhere? Perhaps she had once lived on Boulevard Voltaire, grown used to her local tradesmen, and remained faithful to them?

The young man with the slight build, to his right, was smoking a pipe that was too short in the stem and too large in the bowl, badly balanced, thus forcing him to clamp his teeth. Young people nearly always choose a pipe both too short and too heavy.

The passengers standing on the platform were packed tightly together. The woman ought to have sat inside. In a fishmonger's in Rue du Temple, he spotted some whiting. He hadn't eaten whiting for ages. Why did whiting, too, all of a sudden take on a springlike quality?

Everything was springlike, like his own mood, and it was just too bad if the woman with the chicken was sullenly staring ahead of her, a prey to problems beyond the ken of the common mortal.

"Sorry. . . ."

"Don't mention it. . . ."

He hadn't the courage to say:

"Instead of making everybody out here miserable, why don't you take that wretched string bag of yours and go and sit inside?"

He read the same thoughts in the blue eyes of a large man wedged between him and the conductor. They understood one another. So did the conductor, who imperceptibly shrugged his shoulders. A sort of freemasonry, between men. It was amusing.

The stalls, especially those with vegetables and fruit, were overflowing onto the sidewalks. The green and white bus carved its way through the crowd of cleaning women, secretaries, and clerks hurrying to work. Life was good.

Another jolt. That bag again, with its hard lump at the bottom, potatoes or something of the sort. As he stepped back, he in turn jostled somebody behind him.

"Sorry. . . ."

He also mumbled the word, tried to turn around, and saw the face of a youngish man on which he read an emotion he did not understand.

He must have been less than twenty-five years old; he was bareheaded, with disheveled brown hair, and unshaven. He looked like someone who had not slept all night and who had just been through a trying or painful experience.

Threading his way to the platform step, he jumped from the bus as it was moving. It was at the corner of Rue Rambuteau, not far from the Central Market, the powerful smell of which hung in the air. The man walked fast, turned around as if he were apprehensive about something, then was swallowed up in Rue des Blancs-Manteaux.

For no precise reason, Maigret suddenly put his hand to his hip pocket where he kept his wallet.

He just stopped himself from starting off in his turn and leaping from the bus, for the wallet had vanished.

He had reddened, but he managed to keep his head. Only the big man with blue eyes appeared to have noticed anything amiss.

Maigret smiled ironically, not so much because he had just been the victim of a pickpocket as because it was quite impossible to catch him, and all because of the spring, and the champagne sparkle in the air, which he had begun breathing the day before.

Another habit, a mania, which dated back to his infancy: shoes. Every year, with the first day of fine weather, he bought himself a new pair of shoes, as light as possible. This had occurred the day before.

And this morning he was wearing them for the first time. They pinched. It was torture just to walk the length of Boulevard Richard-Lenoir, and it had been a relief to reach the bus stop on Boulevard Voltaire.

He would have been quite unable to pursue his thief. And anyway the latter had had time to lose himself in the narrow streets of the Marais.

"Sorry. . . ."

Her again! That woman with her shopping! He just managed to stop himself from snapping at her:

"Will you kindly take yourself off with your potatoes and leave us in peace."

But all he did was nod and smile.

In his office, too, there was the same light as he remembered from those first days with a haze hanging over the Seine, less dense than mist, made up of thousands of tiny brilliant, living particles, peculiar to Paris.

"How are things, Chief? Anything doing?"

Janvier was wearing a light suit which Maigret had never seen before. He, too, was celebrating spring early, for it was only the fifteenth of March.

"Nothing. Or rather, yes, there is something. I've just been robbed."

"Your watch?"

"My wallet."

"In the street?"

"In the back of a bus."

"Did it have much money in it?"

"About fifty francs. I seldom carry more."

"And your papers?"

"Not only my papers, but my badge too."

That famous badge of the Police Department, the nightmare of all Inspectors. In theory they should have it always with them, to identify them as Crime Squad officers.

It was a handsome silver badge, or to be more precise plated copper, for with age the thin silver coating wears through to a reddish metal underneath.

On one side the badge showed the Republic's Marianne with her Phrygian cap, the letters. "R.F." and the word "Police" outlined in red enamel.

On the reverse were the arms of Paris, a serial number, and, engraved in small lettering, the holder's name.

Maigret's badge had the number 0004, number 1 being reserved for the Prefect, number 2 for the Director-General of the Police Department, and number 3, for some obscure reason, for the Head of the Special Branch.

Some officers hesitated to carry their badges in their pockets, because the same regulation also provided for suspension of one month's salary in case of loss.

"Did you see the thief?"

"Very clearly. A young fellow, thin, tired-looking, with the eyes and complexion of a person who hasn't slept."

"Did you recognize him?"

When he had worked on the beat, Maigret knew all the pickpockets by sight, not only the ones from Paris, but those who came from Spain or London for the big fairs or open-air festivals.

It is a fairly closed profession, with its own hierarchy. The top operators bestir themselves only when it is worth their while, and they do not think twice about crossing the Atlantic for a world exhibition or, for example, the Olympic Games.

Maigret had lost sight of them somewhat. He was ransacking his memory. He was not making a tragedy out of the incident. The lightness of the morning was still affecting his mood and, paradoxically, he laid all the blame on the woman with the shopping bag.

"If she hadn't been constantly jostling me . . . Women ought to be banned from bus platforms. . . . Especially when she didn't even have the excuse of wanting to smoke. . . ."

He was more annoyed than angry.

"Are you going to look for him in the files?"

"That's what I have in mind."

He spent nearly an hour examining photographs, front view and profile, most of them pickpockets. There were some he had arrested twenty years before, and who after that passed through his office again ten or fifteen times, almost becoming old friends.

"You again?"

"One has to live. And you, you're still there, Chief. It's quite a while since we last met, isn't it?"

Some were well dressed and others, the shabby ones, dossed down in junkyards, the steps of Saint-Ouen, and the Métro corridors. None of them remotely resembled the young man on the bus, and Maigret knew in advance that his search would be a waste of time.

A professional doesn't have that tired, anxious look. He works only when he knows his hands won't start to tremble. And anyway they all knew Maigret's face and profile, if only from seeing it in the newspapers.

He went down to his office again, and when he ran into Janvier he gave a shrug.

"You didn't find him?"

"I'd swear he's an amateur. I even wonder if he knew, a minute earlier, what he was going to do. He must have seen my wallet sticking out. My wife never stops telling me I oughtn't to carry it in that pocket. He must have thought of it when there was a jolt and those confounded potatoes almost knocked me over. . . ."

His tone changed.

"What's new this morning?"

11

"Lucas has got flu. The Senegalese was killed in a *bistrot* on Porte d'Italie. . . ."

"Knife?"

"Of course. Nobody's able to give us a description of the assailant. He came in around one o'clock in the morning, just as the boss was going to close down. He took a few steps in the direction of the Senegalese, who was having a last drink, and he struck so fast that . . ."

Routine. Someone would finally turn him in, maybe in a month, maybe in two years. Maigret went to the Director's office for the daily conference, and he was careful not to mention his little adventure.

The day promised to be a quiet one. Some red tape. Some papers to sign. Routine matters.

He went home for lunch and scrutinized his wife, who didn't talk to him about her driving lesson. For her it was a little as if, at her present age, she had gone back to school. She felt some pleasure, a certain pride even, but also some embarrassment.

"Well then, you didn't drive up onto the sidewalk?"

"Why do you ask me that? You'll give me an inferiority complex. . . ."

"On the contrary. You'll make an excellent driver and I can hardly wait for you to drive me along the banks of the Loire. . . ."

"That won't be for at least another month."

"Is that what the instructor says?"

"The examiners are getting more and more strict and it's best not to be failed the first time. Today we went on the outer boulevards. I would never have believed there was so much traffic on them, or that people drove so fast. Anybody would think . . ."

Imagine, they were eating chicken, as, no doubt, they would be doing in the house of the woman on the bus.

"What are you thinking about?"

"My pickpocket."

"Did you arrest a pickpocket?"

"I didn't arrest him, but he relieved me of my wallet."

"With your badge?"

She, too, thought of it at once. A serious hole in the budget. True, he would get a new badge without the copper showing through.

"Did you see him?"

"As plainly as I see you."

"An old man?"

"A young one. An amateur. He looked as if . . ."

Maigret was thinking about it more and more, without really wanting to. The face, instead of becoming blurred in his memory, was becoming clearer. He was re-capturing details which he was unaware he had recorded in the first place, such as the fact that the unidentified man had thick eyebrows forming an absolute hedge above his eyes.

"Would you recognize him?"

He thought about it more than a dozen times during the course of the afternoon, lifting his head and staring at the window as though some problem were puzzling him. There was something about the episode, the face, the getaway, that wasn't quite natural; he didn't know just what.

Each time it seemed that a new detail, which would convey something to him, was on the point of coming back, then he would turn again to his work.

"Good night, boys. . . ."

He left at five minutes to six, when there were still half a dozen Inspectors left in the next office.

"Good night, Chief. . . ."

They went to the movies. In a drawer he had found his old brown wallet, too large for his hip pocket, so he put it in his coat.

"If you'd kept it in that pocket . . ."

They went home arm in arm, as usual, and the air was still warm. Even the smell of gasoline was not disagreeable that evening. It, too, was part of the spring in the air, in the same way as the smell of melting tar is part and parcel of summer.

In the morning he found the sun still there and had the window open for his breakfast.

"It's funny," he said. "There are women who go halfway across Paris in a bus to do their shopping. . . ."

"Perhaps because of the T.V. sales guide. . . ."

He looked at his wife with a puzzled frown.

"Every night they tell you on television where you can get the best values. . . ."

It had never occurred to him. It was as simple as that. He had wasted hours on a little problem which his wife had solved in an instant.

"Thank you."

"Does that help you?"

"It saves me having to go on thinking about it."

He added, philosophically, grabbing his hat:

"One doesn't think about the things one wants to. . . ."

The mail was waiting for him at the office; on top of the pile there was a large brown envelope on which his name, his rank, and the Quai des Orfèvres address were written in block capitals.

He knew before he opened it. It was his wallet, being returned. And a moment later he discovered that there was nothing missing, neither the badge, nor the papers, nor the fifty francs.

Nothing else. No message. No explanation.

It irked him.

It was just after eleven when the telephone rang.

"There's someone who insists on speaking to you personally but refuses to give his name, Chief Inspector. It seems you are expecting the call and would be angry if I didn't put it through. What do I do?"

"All right, put it through. . . ."

Using one hand to strike a match to relight his pipe, he said:

"Hello!"

There was a longish pause, and Maigret might have thought he had been cut off if he hadn't heard breathing at the other end of the line.

"Hello!" he said again.

Another silence, then:

"It's me. . . ."

A man's voice, quite deep, but judging by the tone it might have been a child hesitating before confessing to an act of disobedience.

"My wallet?"

"Yes."

"Didn't you know who I was?"

"Of course. Otherwise . . ."

"Why are you telephoning?"

"Because I've got to see you. . . ."

"Come to my office."

"No. I can't go to Quai des Orfèvres."

"Are you known here?"

"I've never set foot inside the door."

"What are you afraid of?"

Because the anonymous voice betrayed a note of fear.

"It's a private matter."

"What's private?"

"What I wanted to see you about. This solution occurred to me when I saw your name on the badge."

"Why did you steal my wallet?"

"Because I needed money at once."

"And now?"

"I've changed my mind. I'm still not quite sure about it. The best thing would be for you to come as quickly as possible, before I change my mind. . . ."

There was something unreal about this conversation, in the voice, and yet Maigret was taking it quite seriously.

"Where are you?"

"Are you coming?"

"Yes."

"Alone?"

"Do you insist that I come alone?"

"Our conversation must remain private. Do I have your word?"

"It depends."

"On what?"

"On what you have to tell me."

Another silence, heavier now than the one at the start.

"I want you to give me a chance. After all it was I who called you. You don't know me. You have no way of tracing me. If you don't come, you'll never know who I am. So it's worth, to you . . ."

He could not find the word.

"A promise?" Maigret prompted him.

"Wait. Once I've spoken to you, you must

give me five minutes to disappear if I ask for it . . ."

"I can't make any promises without knowing more about it. I am a police officer and . . ."

"If you'll only believe me, it'll be all right. If you don't believe me, or if you have any doubts, you could manage to look the other way, to give me time to leave, and afterwards you can call up your men. . . ."

"Where are you?"

"Do you agree"

"I'm prepared to come and join you."

"Under my conditions?"

"I shall be alone."

"But you promise nothing?"

"No."

It was impossible for him to act otherwise, and he awaited the reaction of the other man with some anxiety. The latter was in a public telephone booth, or in a café, because he could hear the noise in the background.

"Have you made up your mind?" said Maigret, growing impatient.

"Now that I've come this far . . . What the newspapers say about you gives me hope. Are they true, those stories?"

"What stories?"

"That you are capable of understanding things which normally policemen and judges don't understand and that, in certain cases, you've even . . ."

"Even what?"

"Perhaps it's a mistake for me to talk so much. I don't know any longer. Have you ever been known to turn a blind eye?"

Maigret preferred not to answer.

"Where are you?"

"A long way from Police Headquarters. If I tell you now you'll have time to have me arrested by the local police. You've got my description, one quick call . . ."

"How do you know I saw you?"

"I turned around. Our eyes met, as you know. I was very scared."

"Because of the wallet?"

"Not just that. Listen. Drive to the bar called the Métro, on the corner of Boulevard de Grenelle and Avenue de La-Motte-Picquet. That'll take you about half an hour. I will call you there. I won't be far off and I will be with you almost immediately."

Maigret opened his mouth, but the other man had hung up. He was as curious as he was angry, for it was the first time a complete stranger had treated him with such lack of deference, not to say high-handedness.

And yet he could not bring himself to feel any hostility. Throughout their jerky conversation he had sensed an anguish, a desire to find a satisfactory way out, a need to come face to face with the Chief Inspector who, in the unknown man's eyes, figured as his only hope of salvation. All because he had stolen his wallet, without realizing who he was!

"Janvier! Have you got a car downstairs? I want you to drive me to Boulevard de Grenelle."

Janvier was surprised, there being no case at present in that area.

"A private meeting with the character who lifted my wallet."

"Have you got it back?"

"The wallet, yes, in this morning's mail."

"And your badge? That would surprise me, because it's the sort of thing anybody would like to keep as a souvenir."

"My badge was there, my papers, the money. . . ."

"Was it a joke?"

"No, on the contrary, I have the impression that it's something very serious.

21

My pickpocket has just called up to say he's waiting for me."

"Shall I come too?"

"As far as Boulevard de Grenelle. Then you must stay behind because he wants to see me alone."

They followed the riverbank as far as the Bir-Hakeim bridge. Maigret was silently contemplating the Seine as it flowed by. There were street repairs going on everywhere, with barriers and detours, just as there had been in the first year he came to Paris. In fact, it used to happen in ten-year cycles, each time that Paris started once again to suffocate.

"Where shall I drop you?"

"Here."

They were at the corner of Boulevard de Grenelle and Rue Saint-Charles.

"Shall I wait?"

"Wait for half an hour. If I'm not back by then, go to the office, or have lunch."

Janvier was curious, too, and watched the Chief Inspector's retreating silhouette with a quizzical look.

The sun was hitting the sidewalk where hot gusts and colder gusts alternated, as if the air as a whole had not yet had time to settle down to its spring temperature.

A small girl was selling violets outside a restaurant. From a long way off, Maigret spotted the corner bar, headed by the words *Le Metro,* which would be lit up in the evening. It was just an ordinary place, without personality, one of those tobacco bars where one goes to buy cigarettes, or have a drink at the counter, or else to sit and wait for a date.

His eyes traveled around the place, which had only about twenty tables on either side of the room, most of them unoccupied.

Of course his pickpocket of the day before was not there; the Chief Inspector went and sat down at the very back of the room, by the window, and ordered a beer.

In spite of himself he kept an eye on the door and the people who came up to it, pushed it open, went up to the cash desk behind which the cigarettes were stacked on the shelves.

He was beginning to wonder whether he had not been too gullible when he recognized the silhouette on the sidewalk, then the face. The young man was not looking in his direction; he headed for the copper bar, put his elbows on it, and ordered:

"A rum. . . ."

He was agitated. His hands moved restlessly. He didn't have the nerve to turn around, and he was waiting impatiently to be served, as he needed a drink badly.

Seizing his glass, he gestured to the bartender not to put the bottle back.

"Give me another. . . ."

This time, he turned in Maigret's direction. He knew, before going in, where he was. He must have spotted him from outside, or through the window of a nearby house.

He had an air of apology, as if saying that he had no choice, that he was coming over right away. With still trembling hands he counted out some small change and put it on the counter.

Finally he went over, seized a chair, and collapsed into it.

"Do you have a cigarette?"

"No. I only smoke . . ."

"A pipe, I know. I haven't got any cigarettes, or any money to buy them."

"Waiter! A pack of . . . What's your brand?"

"Gauloises."

"A pack of Gauloises and a glass of rum."

"No more rum. It makes me sick. . . ."

"A beer?"

24

"I don't know. I didn't eat anything this morning . . ."

"A sandwich?"

There were several platters at the bar.

"Not just yet. I'm all in knots. You wouldn't understand. . . ."

He was well dressed, in gray flannel trousers and a tartan sports jacket. Like many young men, he was wearing no tie but had on a polo shirt.

"I don't know if you're at all the way one imagines you. . . ."

He was not looking Maigret in the face, but shot him a series of sidelong glances before fastening his gaze once more on the floor. It was tiring to follow the incessant movement of his long, thin fingers.

"Weren't you surprised to get the wallet?"

"After thirty years of detective work, one isn't easily surprised."

"And to find the money intact?"

"You needed it badly, didn't you?"

"Yes."

"How much did you have in your pocket?"

"About ten francs."

"Where did you sleep last night?"

"I didn't sleep. I didn't eat either. I drank with my ten francs. You just saw me spend the last of the change. There wasn't enough left to get drunk on. . . ."

"And yet you live in Paris," Maigret observed.

"How do you know?"

"And in this very area."

There was nobody at the nearby tables, so they just spoke in muted voices. The sound of the door opening and shutting, nearly always for tobacco or matches, could be heard.

"But you didn't go home. . . ."

The other was silent for a moment, as on the telephone. He was pale, exhausted. One could feel that he was making a desperate effort to respond and trying, warily, to smell out any traps that might be set for him.

"Just as I thought," he grumbled, finally.

"What did you think?"

"That you would guess, that you'd get it more or less right the first time, and that once you were on the scent . . ."

"Go on. . . ."

He grew angry all of a sudden, raised his voice, forgetting that he was in a public place.

"And that once you were on the scent, I'd had it!"

He looked at the door, which had just

opened, and for one moment the Chief Inspector thought he was going to bolt. He must have been tempted. There was a fleeting gleam in his dark pupils. Then he reached out to his glass of beer and emptied it in one gulp, his eyes fixed on the other man over his glass, as though sizing him up.

"Is that better?"

"I don't know yet."

"Let's get back to the wallet."

"Why?"

"Because that's what made you telephone me."

"Anyway, there wasn't enough."

"Not enough money? What for?"

"To get away. . . . To go anywhere, Belgium or Spain . . ."

And, overcome once again by suspicion:

"Did you come by yourself?"

"I don't drive. One of my inspectors brought me and he's waiting at the corner of Rue Saint-Charles."

The man lifted his head with a jerk.

"Did you identify me?"

"No. Your photograph isn't in our files."

"So you did have a look?"

"Of course."

"Why?"

"On account of my wallet, and even more on account of my badge."

"Why did you stop at the corner of Rue Saint-Charles?"

"Because it's just nearby and we were passing that way."

"You haven't had any report?"

"What about?"

"Nothing has happened in Rue Saint-Charles?"

Maigret was hard put to it to follow the successive expressions registered on the young man's face. Seldom had he seen anyone so anxious, so tortured, clinging to God knew what last hope.

He was afraid, obviously. But of what?

"Didn't the local police station alert you?"

"No."

"Do you swear that?"

"I only swear in the witness box."

The other's eyes seemed to bore into him.

"Why do you think I asked you to come?"

"Because you've got yourself into a mess and you don't know how to get out of it."

"That's not true."

The voice was sharp. The unidentified man raised his head, as though relieved.

"It's not I who am in trouble, and that— witness box or no witness box—I can swear to without hesitation. I'm innocent, do you understand!"

"Not so loud. . . ."

He glanced around. A young woman was putting some lipstick on, looking at herself in a mirror, then she turned toward the sidewalk in the hope of seeing the person she was waiting for. Two middle-aged men, hunched over a table, were talking in undertones, and from a few words he guessed at rather than actually heard, Maigret gathered the subject was racing.

"Tell me, instead, who you are and what you claim to be innocent of."

"Not here. Presently. . . ."

"Where?"

"At my house. May I have another beer? I will be in a position to pay you back presently, unless . . ."

"Unless what?"

"Unless her bag . . . Well . . . A beer?"

"Waiter! Two beers. . . . And the check."

The young man dabbed himself with a handkerchief which was still moderately clean.

"You're twenty-four?" the Chief Inspector asked him.

"Twenty-five."

"Have you been in Paris long?"

"Five years."

"Married?"

He was avoiding questions that would be too personal, too inflammatory.

"I was. Why do you ask that?"

"You don't wear a ring."

"Because I couldn't afford one when I got married."

He was lighting a second cigarette. He had smoked the first one inhaling deeply, and only now did he pause to savor the tobacco.

"The fact is, all the precautions I took are useless."

"What precautions?"

"As far as you are concerned. You've got me, neatly tied up, whatever I do. Even if I tried to make a break, now that you've seen me and know I come from around here . . ."

He had a bitter, ironical smile, an irony directed against himself.

"I always overdo everything. Your inspector with the car, is he still at the corner of Rue Saint-Charles?"

Maigret consulted the electric clock. It pointed to three minutes to twelve.

"Either he's just left, or else he's on the point of leaving; I told him to wait half an hour for me, and if I'm not back by then, to go and have lunch."

"It doesn't matter, does it?"

Maigret didn't answer, and when his companion rose, he followed. The two of them set off toward Rue Saint-Charles, on the corner of which stood a fairly new and modern apartment building. They took the pedestrian crossing and started down the street, but only covered about thirty yards.

The young man had stopped in the middle of the sidewalk. An open door led into the courtyard of the big building giving on Boulevard de Grenelle; under an arch, motorcycles and baby carriages were parked.

"Is this where you live?"

"Listen, Inspector . . ."

He was paler and more nervous than ever.

"Have you ever trusted a person, even when all the evidence was against him?"

"I've been known to."

"What do you think of me?"

"That you are rather complicated and there are too many pieces missing for me to judge you."

"Because you will be judging me?"

"That's not what I mean. Let's say, form an opinion."

"Do I look the part of a villain?"

31

"Certainly not."

"Or a man capable of . . . No . . . Come on . . . Best get it over quickly."

He took him into the courtyard and led him toward the left-hand wing, where, on the ground floor, a line of doors could be seen.

"That's what they call studios," he grumbled.

And he took a key from his pocket.

"If you force me to go in first . . . I'll do it. But if I pass out . . ."

He pushed the polished oak door. It opened onto a minute hall. An open door on the right revealed a bathroom with a hip bath. It was in a mess. Towels were strewn over the tiling.

"Open it, will you?"

The young man was indicating to Maigret the door directly in front, which was shut, and the Chief Inspector did what he asked.

His companion did not bolt. But the smell was nauseating, in spite of the open window.

Beside a couch which opened up into a bed at night, a woman was stretched on the multicolored Moroccan carpet, and bluebottles were circling and buzzing in the air around her.

——TWO

"HAVE you got a telephone?"

It was a ridiculous question, which Maigret put automatically, because he could see one on the floor in the middle of the room, about a yard from the body.

"I beg you . . ." muttered his companion, leaning for support against the door frame.

He was already at the end of his tether. For his part, the Chief Inspector was not sorry to leave this room where the smell of death had become unbearable.

He propelled the young man out, closed the door again behind him, and paused for a moment to readjust himself to the real world.

Children were returning from school, swinging their satchels, making their way to the various apartments. Most of the windows in the vast building were open. Several radios could be heard simultaneously, voices, music, women calling their husbands or their sons. On the first floor a canary fluttered about in its cage, and at another window there was some laundry hanging out to dry.

"Are you going to be sick?"

His companion shook his head but still did not dare open his mouth. He was clutching his chest with both hands, deathly pale, on the point of collapsing to judge by the near-convulsive movement of his fingers and the uncontrollable trembling of his lips.

"Take your time. . . . Don't try to talk. . . . Would you like to come and have a drink in the café on the corner?"

Again a shake of the head.

"It's your wife, isn't it?"

The man's eyes said that it was. Finally he opened his mouth to take a deep breath, but succeeded only after a long pause, as though his nerves were clamped in knots.

"Were you there when it happened?"

"No. . . ."

In spite of everything, he had managed to utter the single syllable.

"When did you see her last?"

"The day before yesterday. Wednesday. . . ."

"In the morning? In the evening?"

"Late in the evening. . . ."

They were walking, automatically, across

the great sunbathed courtyard, all around which people were leading their daily lives in different compartments in the building. Most of them were eating, or just about to do so.

Fragments of sentences reached their ears:

"Did you wash your hands . . . ?"

"Watch out. . . . It's very hot."

Kitchen smells, particularly leeks, mingled here and there with the already spring-like air.

"Do you know how she died?"

The young man nodded, short of breath once again.

"When I got back . . ."

"One moment . . . You left the apartment late on Wednesday evening. Keep walking. Standing still won't do you any good. What time, roughly?"

"Eleven o'clock. . . ."

"Was your wife still alive? Was she in her dressing gown when you left her?"

"She hadn't undressed yet. . . ."

"Do you work at night?"

"No. I was going out to scurry up some money. . . . We were broke. . . ."

They both glanced unthinkingly at the open windows as they passed by, and at some of them the occupants stared back,

35

doubtless wondering what they were doing, walking about in this fashion.

"Where were you going to look for the money?"

"Friends' houses. . . . Anywhere. . . ."

"Did you succeed?"

"No. . . ."

"Did any of these friends see you?"

"At the Old Wine Press, yes. . . . I still had about thirty francs in my pocket. I looked in at various places where there was a chance of finding somebody I knew. . . ."

"On foot?"

"In my car. . . . I didn't abandon it until I ran out of gas, at the corner of Rue François-Premier and Rue Marboeuf. . . ."

"What did you do then?"

"I walked. . . ."

The young man Maigret had on his hands was exhausted, his nerves raw, like a person who has been flayed alive.

"How long have you been without food?"

"Yesterday I ate two hard-boiled eggs in a *bistrot*. . . ."

"Come with me. . . ."

"I'm not hungry. . . . If you are thinking of giving me lunch I may as well tell you right away . . ."

Maigret was not listening but made for

Boulevard de Grenelle and went into a small restaurant where there were several unoccupied tables.

"Steak and chips for two," he ordered.

He wasn't hungry either, but his companion was in need of sustenance.

"What's your name?"

"Ricain. François Ricain. . . . Some people call me Francis. . . . It was my wife who . . ."

"Listen, Ricain. I've got to make a couple of telephone calls. . . ."

"To bring your men here?"

"Before I do anything else I've got to call the local Inspector, to let Headquarters know what's happening. Do you give your word you won't budge from here?"

"Where would I go?" Ricain replied bitterly. "In any case you'll arrest me and put me in prison. . . . I won't be able to stand it. . . . I would rather . . ."

He didn't finish, but his meaning was clear.

"A half bottle of Beaujolais, waiter. . . ."

Maigret went to the cashier to get some telephone counters. As he had expected, the local Inspector was out to lunch.

"Do you want me to get a message to him right away?"

"What time will he be back?"

"Around two o'clock. . . ."

"Tell him I'll be waiting for him at half past two in Rue Saint-Charles, by the entrance of the house on the corner of Boulevard de Grenelle. . . ."

At the Public Prosecutor's office, he only got through to a junior clerk.

"A crime has apparently been committed in Rue Saint-Charles. Take down the address. . . . When one of the officers on duty comes back, tell him I will be outside the entrance at a quarter past two. . . ."

Finally Police Headquarters, where Lapointe took the call:

"I'll expect you at Rue Saint-Charles in an hour. Alert Records. . . . Tell them to be at the same address around two o'clock. Tell them to bring something to disinfect a room where the smell is so strong you can't get in. Alert the pathologist. I don't know who's on duty today. See you there. . . ."

He went and sat down opposite Ricain, who had not moved and was looking around as if unable to believe that this commonplace spectacle was real.

It was a modest restaurant. Most of the customers worked in the neighborhood and ate alone, reading newspapers. The steaks were rare and the fried potatoes were crisp.

"What's going to happen next?" asked the young man, automatically picking up his fork. "Did you alert everybody? Is the circus about to start?"

"Not before two o'clock. From now till then, we've got time to chat. . . ."

"I don't know anything. . . ."

"People always think they don't know anything. . . ."

He must not push him. After a few moments, as Maigret was putting a piece of meat in his mouth, François Ricain began, unconsciously, to cut his steak.

He had stated that he would be unable to eat. Not only was he eating, but he drank, and a few minutes later the Chief Inspector had to order a second half bottle.

"Even so you can't possibly understand. . . ."

"Of all the things people say, that's the one I've heard most often during my career. But nine times out of ten I have understood. . . ."

"I know. You'll be teaching me to blow my nose next . . ."

"Does it need blowing?"

"It's not a laughing matter. You've seen, as I have . . ."

"The difference being that you had already seen it before. Isn't that right?"

"Certainly."

"When?"

"Yesterday, at about four o'clock in the morning."

"Hold on a minute while I get this straight. The day before yesterday, that's to say Wednesday, you left your apartment at about eleven o'clock in the evening and your wife stayed behind . . ."

"Sophie pressed me to take her too. I made her stay because I don't like begging for money in her presence. It would have looked as if I were using her. . . ."

"Right! You left by car. What sort of car?"

"A Triumph convertible."

"If you needed money so badly, why not sell it?"

"Because I wouldn't have got a hundred francs for it. It's an ancient car I bought secondhand, and it's passed through God knows how many hands. It hardly stands up on its four wheels. . . ."

"You looked for any friends who might

be able to lend you money, and you didn't find any?"

"The ones I found were almost as broke as I was. . . ."

"You returned home, on foot, at four o'clock in the morning. Did you knock?"

"No. I opened the door with my key. . . ."

"Had you been drinking?"

"A certain amount, yes. At night, most of the people I see hang around bars or night clubs. . . ."

"Were you drunk?"

"Not to the point . . ."

"Depressed?"

"I was at my wits' end. . . ."

"Did your wife have any money?"

"No more than I did. There must have been twenty or thirty francs left in her bag."

"Go on. . . . Waiter! Some more chips, please. . . ."

"I found her on the floor. When I went over to her, I saw that half her face had sort of . . . gone. . . . I think I saw brains. . . ."

He pushed his plate away and drank down his fourth glass of wine in gulps.

"I'm sorry. I'd rather not talk about that. . . ."

"Was there a weapon in the room?"

Ricain stopped short, looking narrowly at

Maigret, as though the crucial moment had come.

"A revolver? An automatic?"

"Yes."

"An automatic?"

"Mine. . . . A 6.35 Browning made in Hertal. . . ."

"How did you come to have this weapon in your possession?"

"I was waiting for that question. And you probably won't believe me. . . ."

"You didn't buy it at a gunsmith's?"

"No. I had no reason to buy a gun. . . . One night there were several of us, just friends, in a small restaurant in La Villette. We'd had a lot to drink. . . . We were showing off and pretending to be tough. . . ."

He had reddened.

"Especially me. . . . The others will bear me out. . . . It's a phobia of mine. When I drink, I think I'm really somebody. . . . Some people we didn't know attached themselves to us. You know how those things go on into the small hours. It was in winter, two years ago. I was wearing a sheepskin jacket. Sophie was with me. She had been drinking too, but she never completely loses her head. . . .

"Next day, around noon, when I went

to put on my jacket, I found an automatic in the pocket. My wife told me I'd bought it the night before, in spite of her pleas. . . . I was insisting, apparently, that I absolutely had to kill someone who had a grudge against me. . . . I kept repeating:

" 'It's him or me, you see, old man!' "

Maigret had lit his pipe and was looking at his companion without betraying any sign of what he was thinking.

"Can *you* understand?"

"Go on. . . . We were at Thursday, four A.M. I suppose nobody saw you come home?"

"Of course not."

"And nobody saw you go out again?"

"Nobody."

"What did you do with the weapon?"

"How do you know I got rid of it?"

The Chief Inspector shrugged.

"I don't know why I did it. I realized I'd be accused. . . ."

"Why?"

Ricain looked at his questioner in amazement.

"It's obvious, isn't it? I was the only person with the key. . . . The weapon that was used belonged to me, and stayed in the chest of drawers. . . . We sometimes had fights, Sophie and I. . . . She wanted me to get a steady job."

"What is your profession?"

"If you can call it a profession . . . I'm a journalist, without being attached to any particular paper. . . . In other words I place my copy where I can, mostly movie reviews. I'm also an assistant director, and sometimes a script writer. . . ."

"Did you throw the Browning into the Seine?"

"Just below the Bir-Hakeim bridge. Then I walked . . ."

"Did you go on trying to find your friends?"

"I didn't dare to any longer. Someone might have heard the shot and telephoned the police. I don't know . . . One isn't necessarily logical in moments like that. . . .

"I was about to be hunted down. . . . I would be accused and everything would be against me, even the fact that I had roamed about part of the night. . . . I had been drinking. . . . I was still in search of the first bar to open. . . . When I found one, in Rue Vaugirard, I drank three straight glasses of rum. . . .

"If anybody were to question me, I would be in no fit state to answer. I was sure to get muddled. They would shut me up in a cell. I suffer from claustrophobia, so badly that I cannot travel by subway. . . . The idea of prison, with huge bolts on the door . . ."

"Was it claustrophobia that gave you the idea of running away abroad?"

"You see! You don't believe me!"

"Perhaps I do."

"You have to have been in a situation like mine to know what goes on in one's head. . . . One doesn't work things out logically. I couldn't tell you what route I took. I needed to walk, to get away from the Grenelle neighborhood, where I pictured them already on my track. I remember noticing Montparnasse station, drinking white wine on Boulevard Saint-Michel . . . or perhaps it was in Montparnasse station. . . .

"My idea wasn't so much to run away. . . . It was to gain time, not to be interrogated in the state I was in. In Belgium, or somewhere else, I would have been able to wait. I would have followed the progress of the investigation in the papers. I would have found out details that I don't know about and which would have helped my defense. . . ."

Maigret could not help smiling at such a mixture of astuteness and naïveté.

"What were you doing in Place de la République?"

"Nothing. I wound up there, just as I might have wound up anywhere else. . . . I had one ten-franc note left in my pocket. I let three buses go by."

"Because they didn't have an open platform?"

"I don't know. . . . I swear, Inspector, that I don't know. I needed money to take the train. I got on the platform. There were a lot of people and we were packed tightly together. I saw you from behind. . . .

"At one moment you stepped back and you nearly lost your balance. I noticed the wallet sticking out of your pocket. . . . I grabbed it, without thinking, and when I looked up I saw a woman looking straight at me. . . .

"I can't think why she didn't give the alarm there and then. I jumped from the bus as it was moving. Luckily, it was a very busy street, with a jumble of narrow streets all around it. I ran. . . . I walked. . . ."

"Two pastries, waiter. . . ."

It was half past one. In forty-five minutes, justice would don its usual trappings, and the studio in Rue Saint-Charles would be invaded by officials, while police outside would keep onlookers away.

"What are you going to do with me?"

Maigret didn't answer immediately, for the good reason that he had not yet made up his mind.

"Are you arresting me? I realize you can't do anything else, but I swear to you once more . . ."

"Eat up. . . . Coffee?"

"What are you doing this for?"

"What am I doing that's so extraordinary?"

"You're making me eat, and drink. . . . You aren't pushing me around. On the contrary, you are patiently listening. . . . Surely that's not what you call grilling a person?"

Maigret smiled.

"Not exactly, no. . . . I'm just trying to get the facts into some sort of order."

"And get me talking. . . ."

"I haven't pressed you too much."

"Well, I do feel a bit better. . . ."

He had eaten his pastry seemingly without noticing, and he was lighting a cigarette. A little color had returned to his cheeks.

47

"Only, I couldn't go back there, and see . . . smell . . ."

"How about me?"

"That's your job. It isn't your wife. . . ."

He passed without transition from non-sense to sense, from blind panic to lucid reasoning.

"You're a strange creature. . . ."

"Because I'm straightforward?"

"I'm not anxious, either, to have you getting in my way when the Forensic Department descends, and I'm even less keen on reporters' pestering you with questions.

"When my inspectors arrive at Rue Saint-Charles—in fact, they must be there by now waiting for us—I'll get them to take you to Rue des Orfèvres. . . ."

"To the cells?"

"To my office, where you will wait for me quietly."

"And then? What happens after that?"

"That depends. . . ."

"What do you hope to find out?"

"I have no idea. . . . I have even less idea than you have, because I haven't studied the body closely and I haven't seen the weapon."

This whole conversation had been accompanied by the sound of glasses, knives and forks, the buzz of voices, the bustle of the waiters and the high-pitched tinkle of the cash-register bell.

The far side of the sidewalk was getting the sun, and the shadows of the passers-by were short and squat. Cars, taxis, buses came past, doors were slammed.

On leaving the restaurant the two men paused, as if hesitating. In their corner in the *bistrot*, they had been isolated for quite a time from other people, from the life that flowed by, from familiar noises, voices, and images.

"Do you believe me?"

Ricain put the question without daring to look at Maigret.

"The moment for believing or not believing hasn't come yet. Look! My men are here. . . ."

He could see one of the black cars of the Police Department in Rue Saint-Charles, and the truck of the Records Department, and he recognized Lapointe in the little group chatting on the sidewalk. The big Torrence was there too, and it was to him that the Chief Inspector entrusted his companion.

"Take him to the Quai. Make him wait in my office, stay with him, and don't be surprised if he falls asleep. He hasn't had a wink for two nights."

Shortly after two o'clock, a truck of the Paris City Health Department was seen arriving: Moers and his men did not have the necessary equipment.

Now there were groups of men in the courtyard waiting outside the studio door; the bystanders, kept at a distance by uniformed police, were observing them attentively.

On one side, Dréville, the Assistant Public Prosecutor, and Camus, the Magistrate, were chatting with Chief Inspector Piget of the XVth *Arrondissement*. All of them had come straight from lunch, and a pretty substantial meal at that, and as the work of disinfecting dragged on, they kept glancing at their watches.

The pathologist was Dr. Delaplanque, relatively new to the job; Maigret liked him and was now asking a few questions. Despite the smell and the flies, Delaplanque had not hesitated to go into the room and make a preliminary examination.

"I'll be able to tell you a bit more presently. You mentioned a 6.35 pistol, which surprises me—I would have been willing to bet the wound was made with a heavier weapon."

"How about the range?"

"On first inspection, there was no burn, no powder marks. Death was instantaneous, or almost, as the woman lost very little blood. Who is she, by the way?"

"The wife of a young journalist."

For everybody, Moers and the experts from Records, it was routine work carried out without personal feeling. They had all heard one of the men from the Health Department exclaiming, as he went into the room: "My, that dame stinks!"

Some of the women had babies in their arms, others, strategically placed to see everything without having to move, were leaning on their elbows at their windows, and their comments were bandied from apartment to apartment.

"Are you sure it isn't the taller one?"

"No, I don't know the tall one. . . ."

They were referring to Lourtie. It was Maigret the two women were watching for.

"There he is! The one smoking the pipe. . . ."

"Two of them are smoking pipes."

"Not the very young one, silly. The other

one. . . . He's going up to the men from the Ministry."

Dréville, the Assistant Prosecutor, was asking the Chief Inspector:

"Have you got any idea what it's all about?"

"The dead woman is a girl of twenty-two, Sophie Ricain, maiden name Le Gal, born in Concarneau, where her father is a watchmaker."

"Has he been notified?"

"Not yet. I'll see to that presently."

"Married?"

"For three years, to François Ricain, a young journalist who dabbles in the movies and is trying to make his way in Paris. . . ."

"Where is he?"

"In my office."

"Do you suspect him?"

"Not so far. He's in no condition to attend the Coroner's investigation, and he'd only get in our way."

"Where was he when the crime was committed?"

"Nobody knows the time of the crime."

"And you, Doctor, can't you establish it approximately?"

"Not for the moment. Perhaps after the

autopsy, if you can tell me what time the victim had her last meal and what she ate."

"What about the neighbors?"

"You can see some of them watching us. I haven't questioned them yet, but I doubt whether they'll have anything interesting to tell us. As you can see, you can get to these studios without passing the porter's lodge, which is at the Boulevard de Grenelle entrance."

A thankless task. They hung about. They talked aimlessly, and Lapointe followed in his master's steps, not opening his mouth, with the look and the demeanor of a faithful dog.

Now the disinfectant people were bringing out of the studio a large flexible tube, painted gray, which they had taken in a quarter of an hour earlier. The foreman of the team, in a white smock, signaled that they could now go in.

"Don't stay inside the room too long," he advised Maigret. "There's still formol in the air."

Dr. Delaplanque knelt beside the body, which he examined with closer attention than he had done the first time.

"As far as I'm concerned, they can take it away."

"What about you, Maigret?"

Maigret had seen all he had to see, a huddled corpse in a flowered silk dressing gown. A red slipper still clung to one foot. It was impossible to tell from her position in the room what the woman had been doing, or even exactly where she was standing when she was hit by the bullet.

As far as it was possible to judge, the face was fairly ordinary, moderately pretty. Her toenails were painted red but had not been attended to for quite a long time, because the varnish was cracked and the nails were not scrupulously clean.

The clerk was writing away beside his boss, as was the Chief Inspector's secretary.

"Bring the stretcher in. . . ."

They trod on dead flies. One by one, the people who were crowded in the room pulled out their handkerchiefs and put them to their eyes, because of the formol.

The body was taken away, while a respectful silence reigned for a few moments in the courtyard. The men from the Public Prosecutor's office left first, then Delaplanque, while Moers and the experts waited to begin their work.

"Do we look everywhere, Chief?"

"It's best. You never know."

Perhaps they were up against a mystery, and perhaps, on the other hand, it would turn out to be quite straightforward. It is always that way at the start of a case, or nearly always.

His eyes stinging, Maigret pulled open a drawer which contained a wide assortment of objects: an old pair of binoculars, some buttons, a broken pen, pencils, photographs taken during the making of a film, sun glasses, bills. . . .

He would come back when the smell had had time to dissipate, but despite it he still noted the way the studio was decorated. The floor was varnished black, and walls and ceiling were painted a bright red. The furniture, on the other hand, was chalky white, which gave an air of unreality to the whole room. It was like a stage set. Nothing seemed solid.

"What do you think of it, Lapointe? How would you like to live in a room like this?"

"It'd give me nightmares."

They went out. There were still some people lingering in the courtyard, and the police had let them come a little nearer.

"Didn't I tell you it was him? I wonder if he'll be back. They say he does it all himself, and as like as not he'll be questioning all of us."

The speaker, a washed-out blonde with a baby in her arms, was gazing at Maigret with a smile on her face that a film star might have inspired.

"I'm going to leave you Lourtie. Here is the key to the studio. When Moers's men have finished, shut the door again and start questioning the neighbors. The crime, if it is a crime, wasn't committed last night, but the night of Wednesday to Thursday. . . .

"Try to find out whether the neighbors heard any noises. Divide up the residents between Lourtie and yourself. Then question the local shopkeepers. There is a stack of bills in the drawer. You'll find the addresses of the stores where they did their shopping. . . .

"One more thing. . . . Will you make sure the telephone is still working? . . . I have a feeling that when I saw it at noon it was off the hook. . . ."

The telephone was working.

"Don't come back to the Quai, you two, without giving me a ring first. Keep your chins up. . . ."

Maigret went off in the direction of Boulevard de Grenelle and vanished into the

Métro. Half an hour later he emerged into the fresh air and the sun, then went back to his office, where François Ricain was waiting patiently, while Torrence was reading a paper.

"Aren't you thirsty?" he asked Ricain, taking off his hat and opening the window a little wider. "Anything new, Torrence?"

"A reporter just phoned."

"I was surprised not to see them over there. Their tip-off system must be badly organized in the XVth *Arrondissement*. It's Lapointe who'll have them around his neck. . . ."

His eyes turned to Ricain, to his hands, and he said to the Inspector:

"Take him to the laboratory, just in case. . . . Have a paraffin test done. It isn't much use anyway, as it's almost two days since the crime was committed, but it will avoid awkward questions. . . ."

They would know, within a quarter of an hour, whether Ricain had powder marks on his fingers. The absence of them would not be conclusive proof that he had not fired the gun, but it would be a point in his favor.

"Hello! . . . Is that you? . . . I'm sorry. . . . Of course. If it hadn't been work, I would have been back for lunch. . . . Yes,

I ate something, beefsteak and chips, with an overexcited young man. . . . I promised myself I'd ring you as we were going into the restaurant, then we got talking, and I must confess I simply forgot. . . . You aren't cross with me, are you? . . . No, I can't tell. . . . We'll have to see. . . ."

That evening he might or might not be home for dinner, he couldn't tell yet. Especially with a young man like François Ricain, who changed his mood within the space of a few seconds.

Maigret would have been hard put to it to formulate an opinion of him. Intelligent, that he certainly was, even keenly so, as some of his answers revealed. At the same time there was a rather naïve, or childish, side to him.

How should he judge him at that moment? He was in a lamentable physical and mental state, a nervous wreck, torn between conflicting emotions.

If he had not killed his wife, and if he really had toyed with the idea of fleeing to Belgium or somewhere else, it revealed a state of total inner confusion which the claustrophobia he suffered from was not by itself enough to explain.

Probably it was he who had thought

up and done the decoration in the studio, the black flooring, the red walls and ceiling, the ghostly-pale furniture which stood out as though floating in space.

It gave the impression that the ground under one's feet was unstable, that the walls were going to advance or recede as in a movie set, that the chest of drawers, the couch, the table, the chairs, were fakes made of papier-mâché.

Did he not himself seem rather a fake? Maigret imagined the faces of the Assistant Prosecutor, or the Magistrate Camus, if they were to read, from beginning to end, the words the young man had spoken, first in the café at La-Motte-Picquet, and later in the little restaurant.

He would have been interested in Dr. Pardon's impression of him.

Ricain came back, followed by Torrence.

"Well?"

"Result negative. . . ."

"I've never fired a shot in my life, except at a fair. I'd have a hard time finding the safety catch. . . ."

"Sit down."

"Have you seen the Magistrate?"

"The Magistrate and the Assistant Prosecutor."

"What have they decided to do? Am I going to be arrested?"

"That's at least the tenth time I've heard you utter that word. . . . Up till now, I would have only one reason to make an arrest—the theft of my wallet—and I haven't brought a charge against you."

"I returned it to you. . . ."

"Precisely. Now we're going to try to clear up one or two things you have told me, and others which I don't yet know about. You may go, Torrence. Tell Janvier to come in. . . ."

A few moments later Janvier was settling down at the far end of the desk and taking a pencil from his pocket.

"Your name is François Ricain. You are twenty-five years old. Where were you born?"

"In Paris, in Rue Caulaincourt."

A bourgeois, almost provincial street, behind the Sacré-Coeur.

"Are your parents still alive?"

"My father. . . . He's a railroad mechanic."

"How long have you been married?"

"A little over three and a half years. Four years ago this June. . . . The seventeenth. . . ."

"So you were twenty-one and your wife was . . ."

"Eighteen. . . ."

"Was your father already a widower?"

"My mother died when I was fourteen. . . ."

"Did you go on living with your father?"

"For a few years. . . . At seventeen I left."

"Why?"

"Because we didn't get on. . . ."

"Was there any special reason?"

"No. I was bored. . . . He wanted me to go with the railroad, like him, and I refused. He thought I was wasting my time reading and studying. . . ."

"Did you pass your *baccalauréat* exam?"

"I left two years before . . ."

"What for? . . . Where did you live? . . . On what? . . ."

"You're rushing me," complained Ricain.

"I'm not rushing you. I'm asking you elementary questions."

"There were different periods. I sold newspapers in the street. Then I was an errand boy in a printing firm in Rue Montmartre. For a while I shared a room with a friend. . . ."

"His name and address. . . ."

61

"Bernard Fléchier. He had a room in Rue Coquillière. . . . I lost track of him."

"What did he do?"

"He drove a delivery truck."

"Next?"

"I worked for six months in a stationer's. I wrote short stories which I peddled to newspapers. One was accepted and I got a hundred francs. . . . The man I dealt with was surprised to see how young I was."

"Did he accept any other stories?"

"No. The others were rejected. . . ."

"What were you doing when you met your wife—I mean the girl who was to become your wife, Sophie Le Gal—that's right, isn't it?"

"I was third assistant director on a movie which the censors have banned, a film about war made by some young people. . . ."

"Did Sophie have a job?"

"Not regularly. She did walk-on parts. She sometimes did a bit of modeling. . . ."

"Was she living alone?"

"In a hotel room, Saint-Germain-des-Prés."

"Love at first sight?"

"No. We slept together, because after one wild party we wound up together in the street at three o'clock in the morning.

She let me take her home. We stayed together for several months, then one fine day we had the idea of getting married. . . ."

"With her parents' consent?"

"They hadn't much to say. She went to Concarneau and came back with a letter from her father authorizing the marriage."

"And you?"

"I went to see my father, also."

"What did he say?"

"He shrugged. . . ."

"Didn't he go to the wedding?"

"No. Just friends, three or four. . . . In the evening we all ate together at the Central Market."

"Did Sophie have any affairs before meeting you?"

"I wasn't the first one, if that's what you mean."

"She didn't live for any length of time with a man who might have been enough in love with her to try to see her again?"

He seemed to be searching in his memory.

"No. We did meet some former friends of hers, but nothing serious. You know, in four years we had time to mix in various different circles. Some people were our friends for six months, then dropped out of sight. Others took their place, and we saw them every now and then. You ask questions as if it was all clear-cut. They're writing down my answers. I've only got to make one mistake, or get muddled up or leave out some details, and you'll jump to God knows what conclusion. . . . You must admit it's not very fair."

"Would you rather be questioned in the presence of a lawyer?"

"Have I the right?"

"If you consider yourself to be a suspect. . . ."

"And you—what do you consider me to be?"

"The husband of a woman who has died, died a violent death. As a young man who panicked and stole my wallet and then returned it to me with its contents. As a very intelligent but not very stable character. . . ."

"If you'd just spent two nights as I have . . ."

"We'll come to that. So, you've held down different jobs, each one for a short time. . . ."

"It was only to earn my living while I was waiting . . ."

"Waiting to do what?"

"To start my career . . ."

"What career?"

He frowned and looked hard at Maigret, as if to make sure there was no trace of sarcasm in his voice.

"I'm still of two minds. . . . Perhaps I'll do both. Anyhow, I want to write, but I don't know if it will be in the form of movie scripts or novels. Directing tempts me, if I can do the whole film myself. . . ."

"Do you mix with movie people?"

"At the Old Wine Press, yes. You can meet people there who are at the bottom rung like myself, but a producer like Monsieur Carus isn't too grand to come and dine with us. . . ."

"Who is Monsieur Carus?"

"A producer, I told you. He lives in the Raphael Hotel, and his office is at 18b Rue de Bassano, off the Champs-Elysées. . . ."

"Has he financed any movies?"

"Three or four. . . . In co-production with the Germans and Italians. He travels a lot. . . ."

"What sort of age is this gentleman?"

"About forty."

"Married?"

"He lives with a young girl, Nora, who has been a model."

"Did he know your wife?"

"Of course. It's a very informal circle. . . ."

"Has Monsieur Carus got plenty of money?"

"He raises it for his movies."

"But he doesn't have a private income?"

"I told you he lives at the Raphael, where he has a suite. . . . It's pretty expensive. At night he goes to the smartest clubs."

"He wasn't the one you were looking for on the night of Wednesday to Thursday?"

Ricain blushed.

"Yes. Him or someone else. . . . Preferably him because he nearly always has wads of bank notes on him."

"Do you owe him money?"

"Yes. . . ."

"A lot?"

"Upwards of two thousand francs. . . ."

"Doesn't he ask for it back?"

"No. . . ."

A very slight change, hard to pinpoint, was taking place in the young man, and Maigret observed him more closely.

But he had to remain cautious, for he was still prepared to retreat into his shell at any moment.

THREE

WHEN Maigret got up, Ricain began to tremble and looked at him apprehensively, still apparently expecting some blow of fate, or a trick. The Chief Inspector went and stood for a moment by the open window, as if to steep himself in reality by watching the passers-by and the cars on the Saint-Michel bridge, and a tug with a big clover-leaf marking on its funnel.

"I'll be right back."

From the Inspectors' room, he asked for the Pathologists' Laboratory.

"This is Maigret. Would you please find out whether Dr. Delaplanque has finished the autopsy."

He had to wait quite a long time before he heard the pathologist's voice on the other end of the line.

"You've called at just the right moment, Inspector. I was going to call you. Have you been able to find out when exactly the young woman had her last meal, and what it consisted of?"

"I'll tell you in a moment. How about the wound?"

"As far as I can judge the shot was fired at a distance of, say, between a yard and a yard and a half."

"From the front?"

"From the side. The victim was standing up. She must have staggered back a step or two before falling on the carpet. The laboratory, which found patches of blood, will confirm this. And another thing. The woman had had a pregnancy which had been terminated toward the third or fourth month by the crudest possible methods. She smoked a lot, but was in quite good health."

"Do you mind holding on a moment?"

He went back to his office.

"Did you have dinner with your wife on Wednesday evening?"

"Around half past eight, at the Old Wine Press."

"Do you remember what she ate?"

"Wait. . . . I wasn't hungry. I just had some cold meat. Sophie ordered a fish soup which Rose recommended, then some beef. . . ."

"No dessert?"

"No. We drank a carafe of Beaujolais. . . . I had some coffee. Sophie didn't want any."

Maigret went into the next room and repeated the menu to Delaplanque.

"If she ate at half past eight, I can put the death at somewhere around eleven o'clock in the evening, because the food was almost completely digested. I'll tell you more after the chemical analysis, but it'll take a few days."

"Did you do the paraffin test?"

"Yes. I saw to that. There wasn't any trace of powder on the hands. You'll get my preliminary report in the morning."

Maigret went back again to his office and arranged the five or six pipes he kept there in order of size.

"I've got some more questions to put to you, Ricain, but I hesitate to do so today. You're worn out and you're only keeping going on your nerves."

"I'd rather get it over with now. . . ."

"As you wish. So, if I've understood you correctly, you've never, up till now, had any steady job or regular income?"

"There are tens of thousands of us in the same boat, I should think. . . ."

"Whom did you owe money?"

"All the shopkeepers. . . . Some of them won't let us have anything any more. . . . I owe another five hundred francs to Maki."

"Who's he?"

"A sculptor, who lives in the same block. He's abstract, but to make a bit of money he does portrait busts every now and then. This had happened a fortnight ago. He made four or five thousand francs and bought us dinner. Over the dessert I asked him to make me a small loan."

"Who else?"

"There's a stack of them!"

"Did you plan to pay them back?"

"I'm sure one day I'll make a lot of money. Most directors and well-known writers began like me."

"Let's turn to something else. Were you jealous?"

"Of whom?"

"I'm referring to your wife. I presume that sometimes some of your friends used to try to make up to her?"

Ricain fell silent, embarrassed, and shrugged his shoulders.

"I don't think you'll be able to understand. You belong to a different generation. . . . We young people don't attach so much importance to these things."

"Do you mean you allowed her to have intimate relations with other people?"

"It's difficult to reply to such a crude question."

"Even so, try."

"She posed in the nude for Maki. . . ."

"And nothing happened?"

"I never asked them."

"And Monsieur Carus?"

"Carus has as many girls as he wants, all the ones who want to get into the movies or television."

"Does he exploit the situation?"

"I believe so. . . ."

"Didn't your wife try to get into the movies?"

"She had a small speaking part three months ago."

"And you weren't jealous?"

"Not in the way you mean."

"You told me Carus had a mistress. . . ."

"Nora."

"Is she jealous?"

"That's not the same thing. Nora is an intelligent woman, and ambitious. . . . She looks down on the movies. What she cares about is becoming Madame Carus and having plenty of money at her disposal."

"Did she get on well with your wife?"

"As well as with anyone. She was condescending to all of us, men and women alike. . . . What are you driving at?"

"Nothing."

"Are you planning to interrogate everybody I was in touch with?"

"Possibly. Someone killed your wife. You say that it wasn't you, and until I have proof to the contrary I'm inclined to believe you.

"An unknown person got into your home on Wednesday evening, when you had just left. This person had no key, which leads one to suppose that your wife let him into the studio without being suspicious."

Maigret was keeping a close eye on the young man, who was becoming visibly impatient, trying to get a word in.

"One moment! Who, among your friends, knew of the existence of the gun?"

"Nearly all of them. In fact, all. . . ."

"Did you occasionally carry it on you?"

"No. But sometimes, when I was in funds, I would ask my friends around. . . . I would buy some cold cuts and salmon and things like that, and everybody brought a bottle of wine or whisky."

"What time did these little parties finish?"

"Late. We drank a great deal. . . . Some-

times people fell asleep and stayed till morning. Occasionally I would play with the gun,
as a joke. . . ."

"Was it loaded?"

Ricain didn't answer at once, and at these
moments it was difficult not to have suspicions about him.

"I don't know."

"Listen. You speak of parties when everyone was more or less drunk. You would
grab a gun, just for fun, and now you tell
me you didn't even know whether it was
loaded. Earlier you told me you didn't know
where the safety catch was. You could have
killed any one of your friends without meaning to."

"It's possible. When one is drunk . . ."

"Were you often drunk, Ricain?"

"Quite often. Not so drunk I didn't
know what I was doing, but I take my
liquor neat, like most of my friends. When
we meet, especially in clubs and cafés . . ."

"Where did you lock up the gun?"

"It wasn't locked up. It was kept in the
top of the chest with old bits of string, nails,
thumbtacks, bills, all the things we couldn't
find a place for anywhere else."

"So that any one of the people who used

to spend the evening with you could have taken the weapon and used it?"

"Yes."

"Do you have any suspicions?"

A moment's hesitation, once again, a sidelong glance.

"No. . . ."

"Nobody was deeply in love with your wife?"

"I was . . ."

Why did he say it with a note of sarcasm in his voice?

"In love but not jealous?"

"I've already explained . . ."

"And Carus?"

"I told you . . ."

"Maki?"

"He's a big brute to look at, but he's as gentle as a lamb and women frighten him. . . ."

"Tell me about the others, the people you saw, the ones you met up with in the Old Wine Press and who used to round off their evenings with you, when you were solvent. . . ."

"Gérard Dramin. He's an assistant director. He was the one I worked with on a script, when I was third assistant on the picture."

74

"Married?"

"At the moment he's living apart from his wife. It isn't the first time. . . . After a few months they always go back to each other again."

"Where does he live?"

"All over the place, always in hotels. He boasts openly of owning nothing except a suitcase and its contents. . . ."

"Are you taking this down, Janvier?"

"I'm with you, Chief."

"Who else, Ricain?"

"A photographer, Jacques Huguet, who lives in the same block as I, in the center building."

"How old?"

"Thirty."

"Married?"

"Twice. Divorced both times. He has one child by his first wife, two by the second. She lives on the same floor."

"Does he live by himself?"

"With Jocelyne, a nice girl, seven or eight months pregnant. . . ."

"That makes three women in his life. Does he still see the first two?"

"The girls get on well together."

"Go on."

"Go on with what?"

"The list of your friends, the regulars at the Old Wine Press."

"They keep changing, as I told you before. There's Pierre Louchard. . . ."

"What does he do?"

"He's over forty, he's a queer, and he runs an antique shop in Rue de Sèvres."

"What does he have in common with your group?"

"I don't know. He's a regular customer at the Old Wine Press. He follows us about. . . . He doesn't talk much, and seems to feel at home with us."

"Do you owe him money?"

"Not much. . . . Three hundred and fifty francs."

The telephone rang. Maigret picked up the receiver.

"Hello, Chief. Lapointe would like a word with you. Shall I put him through to your office?"

"No, I'll come around."

He went back into the Inspectors' room.

"You asked me to call you when we were through, Chief. Lourtie and I have questioned all the neighbors who could have heard anything, especially the women, as most of the men are still at work.

"Nobody remembers a shot. They are ac-

76

customed to noises coming from the Ricains' apartment at night. Several of the tenants had complained to the janitor about it and were planning to write to the landlord.

"Once at about two o'clock in the morning an old lady who was suffering from tooth-ache was standing by her window when she saw a naked girl burst out of the studio and run into the courtyard pursued by a man.

"She wasn't the only one who said that there used to be orgies in the Ricains' studio."

"Did Sophie have visitors when her husband was away?"

"Well, the fact is, Chief, the women I spoke to weren't very precise. The terms that cropped up most often were: savages, people with no manners, or no morals. As for the concierge, she was waiting for their lease to expire to give them notice to quit: they were six months behind with the rent and the landlord had decided to get rid of them if they didn't pay up. What shall I do?"

"Stay at the studio until I get there. Keep Lourtie with you, as I may need him."

He went back to his office, where Janvier and Ricain were waiting in silence.

"Listen to me, Ricain. At this stage, I don't want to ask the Magistrate for a warrant against you. On the other hand, I don't suppose you want to sleep in Rue Saint-Charles tonight."

"I couldn't . . ."

"You haven't got any money. I would rather not see you let loose again in Paris trying to find a friend who'll lend you something."

"What are you going to do with me?"

"Inspector Janvier is going to take you to a small hotel, not far from here, on the Ile Saint-Louis. You can have food sent up to you. If you pass a drugstore or a pharmacy, buy yourself some soap, a razor, and a toothbrush. . . ."

The Chief Inspector gave Janvier a wink.

"I'd rather you didn't go out. Besides, I must warn you that if you should happen to . . ."

"I'll be followed. . . . I realized that. I'm innocent."

"So you said."

"Don't you trust me?"

"It's not my job to trust people. I'm content to wait. Good night."

Alone once again, Maigret paced his office for a few minutes, pausing every now and then in front of the window. Then he picked up the telephone to tell his wife that he would not be home for dinner.

A quarter of an hour later he was back in the subway on his way to Bir-Hakeim. He knocked on the studio door, and Lapointe let him in.

The smell of disinfectant still hung in the air. Lourtie, seated in the only arm-chair, was smoking a small, exceptionally strong cigar.

"Do you want to sit down, Chief?"

"No thank you. I presume you found nothing new?"

"Some photos. Here's one of the Ricains together on the beach. Another in front of their car. . . ."

Sophie wasn't bad-looking. She had that slightly sulky look that is fashionable among young people and a *bouffant* hair style. In the street one might have taken her for any one of thousands with the same mannerisms and the same way of dressing.

"No wine or liquor?"

"A bottle with some dregs of whisky in that cupboard."

An old, nondescript cupboard, like the cabinet and the chairs, but made original by the flat white paint which contrasted with the black floor and red walls.

Maigret, with his hat on, pipe in mouth, pulled open the doors and drawers. Very few clothes, three dresses altogether, cheap, garish. Some trousers, polo shirts. . . .

The kitchenette, next to the bathroom, was scarcely larger than a cupboard, with its gas ring and miniature refrigerator. In the latter he found an opened bottle of mineral water, a quarter of a pound of butter, three eggs, a cutlet in a congealed sauce.

Nothing was clean, neither the clothes nor the kitchen, nor the bathroom in which the dirty laundry was strewn about.

"Nobody called?"

"Not since we've been here."

By now the crime must have found its way into the evening papers, or would be doing so at any moment.

"Let Lourtie go and have a bite, then come back here and settle down as comfortably as possible. All right, Lourtie, old boy?"

"All right, Chief. Am I allowed a nap?"

As for Maigret and Lapointe, they set out on foot for the Old Wine Press.

"Have you arrested him?"

"No. Torrence has taken him off to the Stork, on the Ile Saint-Louis."

It was not the first time that they had put a customer they had been anxious to keep an eye on in there.

"Do you think he killed her?"

"He's both intelligent enough and stupid enough to have done it. On the other hand . . ."

Maigret struggled for words, but could not find them. He had seldom been so intrigued by a person as he was by this François Ricain. At first sight, he was just an ambitious young man of the kind one runs into every day in Paris or any other capital city.

A future failure? He was only twenty-five. Men who later became famous were still pounding the pavement at his age. At moments the Chief Inspector was inclined to trust him. Then, immediately afterwards, he would give a discouraged sigh.

"If I were his father . . ."

What would he do with a son like François? Try to bring him around, guide him back onto the rails?

He decided to go and see the father in Montmartre. Unless he came around to the Police Headquarters of his own accord when he read the papers.

Lapointe, who was walking beside him in

silence, was little more than twenty-five years old. Maigret mentally compared the two men.

"I think it's there, Chief, on the other side of the boulevard, near the Air Terminal subway station."

They found themselves gazing at an entrance door flanked by two worm-eaten wine presses, with heavily curtained windows through which filtered the pink light of the lamps, which were already lit.

It was not time yet for apéritifs, much less for dinner, and there were only two people in the room, a woman, on the customers' side of the bar, perched on a high stool and drinking through a yellowish straw, and the boss on the other, bent over a newspaper.

The lights were pink, the bar was supported by wine presses, the massive tables were covered with checked cloths, and the walls were three-quarters paneled with dark woodwork.

Maigret, walking ahead of Lapointe, frowned as he caught sight of the man with the newspaper, as if he were trying to remember where he had seen him before.

The boss, for his part, raised his head,

but it only took him an instant to recognize the Chief Inspector.

"What a coincidence," he remarked, tapping the still fresh print. "I was just reading that you were in charge of the case."

And, turning to the girl:

"Fernande, meet Chief Inspector Maigret in person. . . . Sit down, Inspector. What can I offer you?"

"I didn't know you had gone into the restaurant business."

"When you begin to get on a bit . . ."

It was true that Bob Mandille must have been about Maigret's age. He was much talked about in the old days, when he used to think up some new stunt every month, walking along the wing of an airplane in flight, parachuting over the Place de la Concorde and landing a few feet from the Obelisk, or leaping from a galloping horse into a racing car.

The movie industry had turned him into one of its most celebrated stunt men after trying in vain to make him a male lead. People had lost count of the accidents he had had, and his body must be a mass of scars.

He had kept his figure and his elegance. There was just a touch of stiffness in his movements, something mechanical. As for his face, it was just a little too smooth, with slightly too regular features, probably the result of plastic surgery.

"Scotch?"

"Beer."

"Same for you, young man?"

Lapointe was not at all pleased to be addressed in this way.

"You see, Monsieur Maigret. I've had enough. The insurance companies tell me I'm too old to be a good risk and all of a sudden they don't want me in the movies any more. So I married Rose and turned publican. . . . You're looking at my hair? Do you remember my picture, when I was scalped by the blades of a helicopter and my head was as bald as an egg? A wig, that's all it is. . . ."

He raised it, gallantly, as if it were a hat.

"You know Rose, don't you? She sang for a long time at the Trianon-Lyrique. Rose Delval, as she was called then. Her real name is Rose Vatan, which didn't sound right on a billboard. . . .

"Well, what do you want to talk about?"

Maigret glanced in the direction of the girl called Fernande.

"Don't worry about her. She's part of the

84

furniture. In two hours she'll be so drunk she won't be able to move and I'll put her into a taxi. . . ."

"You know Ricain of course?"

"Of course. Your health. . . . I only drink water, so excuse me. . . . Ricain comes to dine here once or twice a week."

"With his wife?"

"With Sophie, naturally. It's unusual to see Francis without Sophie. . . ."

"When did you see them last?"

"Wait. . . . What day is it? Friday. . . . They came on Wednesday evening."

"With friends?"

"None of the gang were here that night. Except for Maki, if I'm not mistaken. . . . I seem to remember Maki eating in his corner."

"Did they sit down with him?"

"No. Francis just stuck his head in and asked me if I'd seen Carus and I said no, I hadn't seen him for two or three days."

"What time did they leave?"

"They didn't come in. They must have eaten somewhere else. Where is Francis now? I hope you haven't put him in . . ."

"Why do you ask?"

"I've just read in the paper that his wife

85

was shot dead with a gun and that he's disappeared. . . ."

Maigret smiled. The news release of the local police station, where they didn't know the full story, had misled the reporters.

"Who told you about my restaurant?"

"Ricain."

"So he's not on the run?"

"No."

"Arrested?"

"Not arrested, either. Do you think he would have been capable of killing Sophie?"

"He's incapable of killing anything. If he was going to, it would be himself. . . ."

"Why?"

"Because there are times when he loses his self-confidence and starts hating himself. That's when he drinks. After a few glasses he becomes desperate, convinced that he's a failure who's going to let his wife down."

"Does he pay you regularly?"

"He's run up quite a bill. . . . If I listened to Rose, I'd have stopped giving him credit long ago. For Rose, business is business. True, her job is harder than mine, at the stove all day. . . . She's there now, and she'll still be there at ten o'clock tonight."

"Did Ricain come back that night?"

"Wait. I was busy with a table, later on

86

. . . I felt a draft and I turned to the door. It was open and I thought I saw him there looking for someone. . . ."

"Did he find him?"

"No."

"What time was this?"

"Around eleven o'clock. You were right to press me. It was that evening that he came back a third time, later. . . . Sometimes, when the dinners are finished we stay on for a chat with the regulars. It was past midnight, on Wednesday, when he came back. He stayed by the door and signaled to me to come over. . . ."

"Did he know the customers you were with?"

"No. They were old friends of Rose, theater people, and Rose had joined us, in her apron. Francis is scared stiff of my wife. . . .

"He asked me if Carus had come. I told him he hadn't. And Gérard? . . . Gérard, that's Dramin, who's going to make a name for himself one day in the movies. . . . He hadn't come, either. Then he blurted out that he needed two thousand francs. I made it clear that I couldn't help. A few dinners, all right. A fifty- or a hundred-franc note every now and then when Rose is looking the other way, that I can manage. But two thousand francs . . ."

"He didn't say why he needed it so badly?"

"Because they were going to turn him out of the studio and sell everything he owned. . . ."

"Was it the first time?"

"No, and that's the point. Rose isn't so very wrong: he's a habitual sponger. But not a cynical one, if you see what I mean. He does it in good faith, always convinced that tomorrow or next week he will be signing a big contract. He's so ashamed of asking that one is ashamed of refusing."

"Is he a nervous person?"

"Have you seen him?"

"Of course."

"Nervous or calm?"

"A bundle of nerves."

"Well, I've never seen him any other way. Sometimes it's quite exhausting to watch. He clenches his fists, makes faces, flies into a fury over nothing, or else he's sorry for himself, or gets on his high horse. And yet, you know, Inspector, he's basically sound, and I wouldn't be surprised if he does something one day."

"What do you think of Sophie?"

"They say you mustn't speak ill of the dead. The Sophies of this world, you run into them by the dozen, if you see what I mean. . . ."

And with a glance he indicated the girl sitting at the bar, lost in contemplation of the bottles in front of her.

"I wonder what he saw in her. There are thousands of them, all dressed alike, with the same make-up, dirty feet, worn heels, wandering about in the mornings in slacks too tight for them and living on salads. All hoping to become models or film stars. . . . Jesus! . . ."

"She had a bit part."

"Ah yes, through Walter."

"Who is Walter?"

"Carus. If you totted up the number of girls who have earned their right to a bit part . . ."

"What sort of man is he?"

"Come and have dinner here and you'll probably be able to see for yourself. He sits at the same table one night in two, and there's always someone around to make the most of his hospitality. A producer. . . . You know how it goes. The man who finds the money to start a film, then the money to continue it, and then, after months or years, the money to finish it . . . He's half English and half Turkish, which is an interesting mixture. . . . A decent sort, straight, with a booming voice, always ready to buy a round of drinks and addressing everyone as '*tu*' within five minutes of meeting them."

"Did he call Sophie '*tu*'?"

"He addressed all women as '*tu*' and calls them his baby, his sweetie, or his turtle dove as the fancy takes him."

"Do you think he slept with her?"

"I'd be surprised if he didn't. . . ."

"Wasn't Ricain jealous?"

"I expected that you were coming to that. . . . First of all, Carus wasn't the only one. I would think the others have all had a go at her. I could have, too, if I'd wanted, even though I could almost have been her grandfather. Leaving that aside . . . We had a few rows about that, Rose and I. . . .

"Question Rose and you'll find she hasn't a good word to say for him. She thinks he's a good-for-nothing, living by his wits and playing the big misunderstood act, but in spite of everything really just a little pimp. . . . That's my wife's opinion.

"It's true, of course, that she spends three-quarters of her time in the kitchen, so she doesn't know him as well as I do.

90

"I've tried to make her understand that Francis knew nothing of what was going on."

"Do you believe that?"

The retired acrobat had very pale blue eyes that reminded one of a child's. In spite of his age and his air of experience, he had still preserved a childlike enthusiasm and charm.

"Perhaps I'm a bit naïve, but I trust the boy. There have been times when I haven't been so sure, and then I've almost come around to Rose's way of thinking. . . . But I always come back to my original position: he's really in love. Enough for her to make him believe anything.

"The proof is the way he let himself be treated by her. . . . Some nights, when she had a drop too many, she told him, cynically, that he was nothing but a failure, a zero, that he had no guts, and, if you'll forgive me, no balls either, and that she was wasting her time on a half-portion like him. . . ."

"How did he take it?"

"He would withdraw into his shell, and you could see the beads of sweat on his forehead. Even so, he would force himself to smile:

" 'Come on, Sophie. Come to bed. You're tired. . . .' "

At the back of the room a door opened. A small, very fat woman appeared, wiping her hands on a large apron.

"Well, well! The Chief Inspector. . . ."

And while Maigret was still trying to remember where he could have seen her before, since he had never been a regular customer at the Trianon-Lyrique, she reminded him:

"Twenty-two years ago . . . In your office. You arrested the character who lifted my jewels from my dressing room. I've put on a little weight since then. . . . In fact, it's thanks to those jewels that I was able to buy this restaurant. That's right, isn't it, Bob? But why have you come here?"

Her husband explained, with a gesture toward the newspaper:

"Sophie's dead. . . ."

"Our Sophie, the little Ricain girl?"

"Yes."

"An accident? I'll bet it was him driving and . . ."

"She was murdered."

"What's he saying, Monsieur Maigret?"

"The truth."

"When did it happen?"

"Wednesday evening."

"They had dinner here."

Rose's face had lost not only her good humor, which was her trademark, as it were, but her cordiality.

"What have you been telling him?"

"I've been answering his questions. . . ."

"I bet you haven't had a good word for her. Listen, Inspector, Bob isn't a bad character and we get along quite well together. But on the subject of women, you mustn't listen to him. To hear him you'd think they're all tarts and men are their victims. Now, take this poor girl, for example . . .

"Look at me, Bob. Who was right . . . ? Was it him or her that caught it?"

She paused, glaring at them defiantly, her hands on her hips.

"Make it another, Bob," Fernande mumbled slackly.

And to speed her on her way, Mandille gave her a double portion.

"Were you fond of her, Madame?"

"How can I put it . . . ? She was brought up in the provinces. And moreover at Concarneau, where her father is a watchmaker. I'm sure her mother goes to mass every morning.

"So she comes to Paris and falls in with this gang who thinks they're geniuses because they work in the movies or on television. I've been in the theater myself, which is a far more difficult proposition. I've sung the whole repertoire but I never gave myself airs. While these little nitwits . . ."

"Which ones do you mean in particular?"

"Ricain, for a start. He considered himself the smartest of the lot. . . . When he managed to get an article into a magazine read by a few hundred imbeciles, he imagined he was going to rock the movie world to its foundations. . . .

"He took the girl over. Apparently they actually got married. He might at least have fed her properly, mightn't he? I don't know what they would have done for food if their friends hadn't invited them and if my half-wit of a husband hadn't given them credit. . . . How much does he owe you, Bob?"

"What's it matter?"

"You ass! And here I am, slaving away in the kitchen. . . ."

She was grumbling for the sake of grumbling, which did not prevent her from looking at her husband with a certain tenderness.

"Do you think she was Carus's mistress?"

"As if he needed her! He had enough on his hands with Nora. . . ."

"Is that his wife?"

"No. He wanted to marry her all right, but he has a wife in London and she won't hear of a divorce. Nora . . ."

"What's she like?"

"Don't you know her? That one, now, I wouldn't defend. You can see it isn't just prejudice. What do men see in her, I keep asking myself. . . .

"She's at least thirty, and if you cleaned all her make-up off, you'd probably guess nearer forty. She's thin, it's true, so thin you can count her bones. . . .

"Black and green around the eyes, to make them mysterious, it seems, but it only makes her look like a witch. No mouth, because she hides it under a layer of white stuff . . . And a greenish white on her cheeks. . . . That's Nora for you.

"As for her clothes . . . The other day she turned up in a silver *lamé* pajama affair so tight she had to come into the kitchen to get me to sew up the seam of the trousers. . . ."

"Does she work for the movies?"

"What do you take her for? She leaves that to the young girls who don't count. . . .

Her dream is to become the wife of a big international producer, to be Madame the producer's wife one day."

"You're exaggerating," Mandille sighed.

"Less than you were a moment ago."

"Nora is intelligent, cultivated, much more cultivated than Carus, and without her he probably wouldn't be so successful."

From time to time, Maigret turned to Lapointe, who was listening in silence, motionless by the bar, no doubt dumfounded by what he heard and by the atmosphere of the Old Wine Press.

"Will you stay for dinner, Monsieur Maigret? If there isn't too much of a rush perhaps I'll be able to come over now and then for a chat. There's *mouclade*. . . . I never forget that I was born in La Rochelle, where my mother sold fish, so I know some good recipes. . . . Have you ever eaten *chaudrée fourrassienne?*"

Maigret rattled off, "Soup made of eel, baby sole, and cuttlefish. . . ."

"Have you been there often?"

"To La Rochelle, yes, and to Fourras. . . ."

"Shall I put a *chaudrée* on for you?"

"Please. . . ."

When she had gone off, Maigret grunted: "Your wife doesn't share your opinions about people. If I listened to her I would be arresting François Ricain right away."

"I think you'd be making a mistake."

"Can you suggest anyone else?"

"As the guilty party? No. . . . Where was Francis at the time?"

"Here . . . in this neighborhood. . . . He claims he was running all over Paris looking for Carus or anybody who would lend him some money. Wait now. He mentioned a club. . . ."

"The Zero Club, I'll bet. . . ."

"That's right. Near Rue Jacob."

"Carus often goes there. Some other customers of mine, too. . . . It's one of the latest in-places to go to. The fashion changes every two or three years. Sometimes they don't last as long as that, just a few months. . . . It isn't the first time Francis has been short of money, or that he's been around trying to cadge the odd thousand-franc note, or notes. . . ."

"He didn't find Carus anywhere."

"Did he try his hotel?"

"I imagine so."

"Then he must have been at Enghien. Nora is a great gambler. . . . Last year, at Cannes, he left her alone in the casino, and when he went back for her she had sold her jewels and lost the whole business. . . . Another beer? Wouldn't you prefer an old port?"

"I'd rather have a beer. How about you, Lapointe?"

"A port," Lapointe mumbled, blushing.

"May I use the telephone?"

"In the back on the left. . . . Wait. I'll give you some counters."

He took a handful from the cash drawer and gave them to Maigret without counting them.

"Hello! . . . The Inspectors' room? . . . Who's speaking? Torrence ? . . . Any news? . . . Nobody asked for me? . . . Moers? I'll call him when I've finished with you.

"Have you had a call from Janvier . . . ? He's still at the Stork? The boy's asleep? . . . Good. . . . Yes. . . . Good. . . . You're going to take over from him? . . . Okay, old man. . . . Good night. . . . Keep an eye open, though, even so. . . .

"If he wakes up there's no telling what he may get up to. . . . One second . . . Could you telephone the River Police . . . ?

"Tomorrow morning they should send some frogmen to the Bir-Hakeim bridge. A little above it, a hundred feet at the most, they ought to find a revolver thrown from the bank. . . . Yes. Mention my name. . . ."

He rang off and dialed the laboratory.

"Moers . . . ? I gather you've been trying to get me. . . . You found the bullet in the wall? What . . . ? Probably a 6.35 . . . Well, send it to Gastinne-Renette. . . . It's possible we'll have a weapon to show them tomorrow. . . . And the prints? . . . I expect so. . . . Everywhere . . . on both of them. . . . And of several different people. . . . Men and women. . . . It doesn't surprise me, as they can't have cleaned the place very often. . . . Thank you, Moers. . . . See you tomorrow. . . ."

François Ricain was sleeping the sleep of exhaustion, in a small bedroom in the Ile Saint-Louis, as Maigret was about to settle down to a tasty *chaudrée* in the restaurant where the young couple used to meet their band of friends.

When he left the telephone booth, he could not help smiling as Fernande, who had suddenly come to life again, was making animated conversation with Lapointe, who did not know quite how to react.

FOUR

IT was a strange evening of covert glances, whispers, of comings and goings around the confined floor space, with the pink light and the good smells from the Old Wine Press's kitchen.

Maigret had settled himself with Lapointe near the entrance in a sort of niche where there was a table for two.

"It's the table Ricain and Sophie used to take when they weren't with the others," Mandille had explained.

Lapointe had his back to the room, and every now and then, when the Chief Inspector pointed out something of interest, he would turn around, as discreetly as possible.

The *chaudrée* was good, and it was accompanied by a pleasing Charentes wine not usually sold commercially, the tart wine used to make cognac.

The one-time stunt man comported himself as master of the house, receiving his customers like guests and shepherding them from the door. He joked with them, kissed the women's hands, led them to their tables and, before the waiter had time, handed them the menu.

Almost always he would then come over to Maigret.

"An architect and his wife. . . . They come every Friday, sometimes with their son, who is studying law."

After the architect, two doctors and their wives, at a table for four, also regulars. One of the doctors was expecting a telephone call, and a few minutes later he collected his bag from the hat-check girl and made his apologies to his friends.

Maki the sculptor was eating by himself in his corner with a hearty appetite, helping himself with his fingers more freely than is usually considered good form.

It was eight o'clock when a sallow youth with unhealthy complexion came in and shook hands with him. He did not join him, but went and sat on a bench, spreading a mimeographed manuscript in front of him.

"Dramin," Bob announced. "He usually works while he eats. It's his latest movie script, which he's already had to start all over again two or three times. . . ."

Most of the customers knew one another, at least by sight, and exchanged discreet nods from a distance.

From the descriptions he had been given, Maigret at once recognized Carus and, even more easily, Nora, who would have had difficulty in passing unnoticed.

That evening she was not wearing *lamé* trousers but a dress in a material almost as transparent as cellophane, and so tight that she appeared to be naked.

Of the face, which was whitened like a clown's, one could only actually see the coal-black eyes, underlined not just with black and green but with gold specks which sparkled in the light.

There was something ghostlike about her face, her look, her manner, and the contrast was all the greater compared with the vitality of the portly Carus, with his solidly hewn features and his healthy smiling face.

While she followed Bob to the table, Carus shook hands with Maki, then Dramin, then the one remaining doctor and the two women.

When he in turn had sat down Bob leaned

over to say a few words to him, and the producer's eyes looked around in search of Maigret, coming to rest on him with curiosity. He seemed about to get up to shake hands with Maigret, but first he looked over the menu which had been slipped into his hand, and began discussing it with Nora.

When Mandille came back to Maigret's corner, Maigret expressed his surprise.

"I thought the gang all sat together at the same table?"

"Sometimes they do. Some evenings they stay in their own corners. Occasionally they get together over the coffee. Other days they all sit together. The customers make themselves at home here. We have very little space and we don't encourage . . ."

"Do they all know?"

"They've read the papers, or heard the news on the radio, of course. . . ."

"What are they saying?"

"Nothing. It's given them all quite a shock. Your presence here must make them feel uncomfortable. . . . What will you have after the *chaudrée?* My wife recommends the leg of lamb, which is real *pré-salé* meat. . . ."

"How about it, Lapointe? . . . Right, then, lamb for two. . . ."

"A carafe of red Bordeaux?"

Through the curtains one could see the lights of the boulevard, the passers-by, some walking faster than others, the occasional couple walking arm-in-arm and stopping every few steps to kiss or lovingly look at each other.

Dramin, as Bob had predicted, ate with an eye on his manuscript, every now and then taking a pencil from his pocket to make a correction. He was the only one of Ricain's acquaintances not to appear concerned by the presence of the policemen.

He wore a dark suit, ready-made, a nondescript tie. He might have passed for an accountant or a cashier at the bank.

"Carus is debating whether to come and talk to me or not," Maigret said, who was observing the couple. "I don't know what Nora is whispering to him, but he doesn't agree."

He imagined the other evenings, with François Ricain and Sophie coming in, looking around for their friends, wondering whether anybody would invite them to sit with them, or whether they would have to eat alone in their corner. They must have seemed like poor relations.

"Are you planning to question them, Chief?"

"Not right now. After the lamb."

It was very hot. The doctor who had been called to the invalid's bedside was back already, and from his gesture they gathered that he was complaining that he had been disturbed for nothing.

Where had Fernande, the big girl propped against the bar, got to? Bob must have got rid of her. He was deep in conversation, with three or four customers who had taken her place. They were being very familiar and seemed in high spirits.

"The specter is trying to persuade her man to do something. . . ."

Nora was in fact talking to Carus in a low voice, without taking her eyes off Maigret, giving him advice. What advice?

"He is still hesitating. He is panting to come over and join us, but she's stopping him. I think I'll go over. . . ."

Maigret rose heavily, after wiping his lips with his napkin, and threaded his way between the tables. The couple watched him coming, Nora impassively, Carus with visible satisfaction.

"Am I disturbing you?"

The producer rose to his feet, wiped his mouth too, and held out his hand.

"Walter Carus . . . My wife . . ."

"Chief Inspector Maigret . . ."

"I know. . . . Please sit down. Will you have a glass of champagne with us? My wife drinks nothing else, and I must say I can't blame her for that. Joseph! A champagne glass for the Chief Inspector . . . !"

"Please, go on with your dinner."

"I hardly need tell you I know the reason for your presence. . . . I heard the news just now, on the radio, on my way to the hotel for a shower and a change. . . ."

"Did you know the Ricains well?"

"Quite well. Here we all know one another. . . . He more or less worked for me, in that I've got some money tied up in the film he's working on."

"Didn't his wife play a bit part in another of your pictures?"

"I've forgotten. More likely as an extra."

"Did she mean to make a career of it?"

"I don't think so. Not seriously. . . . At a certain age most girls want to see themselves on the screen."

"Was she talented?"

Maigret had the impression that Nora was kicking Carus under the table, as a warning.

"I must confess to you that I don't know. I don't think she even had a screen test. . . ."

"And Ricain?"

"Are you asking me whether he's talented?"

"What sort of a person is he, from a professional point of view?"

"What would you say, Nora?"

The reply came, icily:

"Zero. . . ."

The remark seemed to fall incongruously and Carus hastened to explain:

"Don't be surprised . . . Nora is a bit psychic. She has a kind of thing which puts her in instant contact with certain people. With others, it has the opposite effect. You can take my word for it or not, but this thing—I can't find any other word to describe it—has often been useful to me in business, even on the Stock Exchange. . . ."

Under the table, the foot was at work again.

"With Francis, contact was never established. . . . Personally, I find him intelligent, gifted, and I'd be willing to bet that he'll go far one day.

"Now take Dramin, for example, buried in his script over there. . . . There's a serious worker for you, who gets the job done as competently as you could wish. I've read some excellent dialogue of his. But unless I'm completely mistaken, he will never be a big-time director. He needs somebody, not only to guide him, but to inject the vital spark. . . ."

He was delighted with the words he had just found.

"The spark! . . . That's what is lacking most of the time, and that's essential, as much in the movies as in television. Hundreds of specialists come up with quite adequate work, a well-constructed story, dialogue that runs smoothly. But almost always, something is missing, and the result is flat and gray. The spark, if you see what I mean . . .

"Well now, you can't count on Francis to provide you with anything solid. His ideas are often preposterous. He has suggested thousands of ideas that would have ruined me. On the other hand, occasionally he has the spark. . . ."

"In what way?"

Carus scratched his nose, comically.

"That's just it . . . You speak like Nora. . . . One evening, after dinner, he will talk with such conviction and such fire that you are sure you have a genius on your hands. Then, next day, you'll realize that what he was saying doesn't make sense. He's young. It'll all come out in the wash. . . ."

"Is he working for you at the moment?"

"Apart from his reviews, which are remarkable, although somewhat too sharp, he doesn't work for anybody. He's full of projects, fusses around with several films at the same time without ever finishing any one of them."

"Does he ask you for advances?"

The feet, under the table, kept up their silent conversation.

"Look, Inspector, our profession isn't like other professions. We are all looking for talent, actors, script writers, and producers . . . It doesn't pay to take a known director who will make you the same film over and over again, and as for stars, it's a question of finding new faces. . . .

"Also we are obliged to gamble on a certain number of promising young people. To gamble modestly, otherwise we'd be ruined overnight. A thousand francs here, a screen test, a word of encouragement . . ."

"In fact, if you lent considerable sums to Ricain it was because you hoped to get the money back someday. . . ."

"Without counting on it too much. . . ."

"And Sophie?"

"I was in no way involved with her career. . . ."

"Did she hope to become a star?"

"Don't make me say more than I already have. She was always with her husband and she didn't talk much. I think she was shy. . . ."

An ironical smile appeared on Nora's pale lips.

"My wife thinks otherwise, and, as I've more confidence in her judgment than I have in my own, don't attach too much weight to my opinions."

"How did Sophie and Francis get along?"

"How do you mean?"

He was feigning surprise.

"Did they seem to you to be very close?"

"You seldom saw one without the other, and I don't ever remember them quarelling in my presence."

Again there was an enigmatic smile on Nora's lips.

"Perhaps she was a bit impatient. . . ."

"In what sense?"

"He believed in his star, in the future, a future which he saw as brilliant, and just round the corner. I suppose that when she married him she imagined she was about to become the wife of a celebrity. Famous and rich . . . Now after more than three years, they were still living from hand to mouth and had nowhere to turn. . . ."

"Did she hold it against him?"

"Not in front of other people, as far as I know."

"Did she have any lovers?"

Nora turned to Carus, as if curious to hear his answer.

"You are asking a question which . . ."

"Why not tell the truth?"

For the first time, she was no longer content with signals under the table, and was breaking her silence.

"My wife is referring to an incident of no importance. . . ."

Nora interrupted, bitingly:

"It depends on whom . . ."

"One night we'd all been drinking. . . ."

"Where was this?"

"At the Raphael. We set off from here. . . . Maki was with us. Dramin, too. Then a photographer, Huguet, who works for an advertising firm. I think Bob came, too. . . .

"At the hotel I had some champagne and some whisky sent up. Later I went into the bathroom and I had to pass through our room, where only the bedside lights were on.

"I found Sophie stretched out on one of the twin beds. Thinking she was ill, I bent over her . . ."

Nora's smile was growing more and more sarcastic.

"She was crying. . . . I had the greatest difficulty in getting a few words out of her. She eventually admitted to me that she was in despair, and wanted to kill herself."

"And how did I find the two of you?"

"I took her, automatically, into my arms, it's true, as I would to console a child. . . ."

"I asked you if she had any lovers. I wasn't thinking particularly of you."

"She posed in the nude for Maki, but I'm sure Maki wouldn't touch the wife of a friend. . . ."

"Was Ricain jealous?"

"You're asking too much of me, Monsieur Maigret. Your good health! . . . It all depends on what you mean by jealousy. . . . He wouldn't have liked to lose his hold over her, and see another man become more important to her. In that sense he was jealous of his friends as well. If, for example, I invited Dramin to come and have coffee at our table without asking him as well, he would sulk for the rest of the week."

"I think I understand."

"Have you had any dessert?"

"I hardly ever touch it."

"Nora doesn't either. Bob! . . . What do you recommend for dessert?"

"A pancake, *flambée*, with maraschino?"

Comically, Carus considered the rounded contours of his stomach.

"What's the difference? Pancakes it is. Two or three. . . . Armagnac rather than maraschino . . ."

All this time, Lapointe had been growing more and more bored in his corner, with his back to the room. Maki was picking his teeth with a match, doubtless asking himself whether his turn would come shortly to face the Chief Inspector across the table.

The doctors' table was the merriest, and from time to time one of the women burst into a piercing laugh which made Nora wince.

Rose abandoned her ovens for a while to make a tour of the tables, wiping her hand on her apron before offering it. Like the doctors, she too was in good spirits, which Sophie's death had done nothing to dampen.

"Well, Walter, you old rascal . . . How come you haven't been seen since Wednesday?"

"I had to fly to Frankfurt, to see a business associate, and from there I went to London."

"Did you go with him, too, dear?"

"Not this trip. I had to go for a fitting. . . ."

"Aren't you afraid to let him travel by himself?"

She moved away with a laugh and stopped by another table, then another. Bob was cooking the pancakes on a grill.

"I gather that Ricain was looking for you during the night? . . ."

"Why would he be looking for me?"

"It was the Inspector who told me just now. He needed two thousand francs urgently. On Wednesday he came around here and asked for you."

"I took the five o'clock plane. . . ."

"He came back twice. He wanted me to lend him the money, but it was too big a loan for me. Then he went on to the club."

"Why did he want two thousand francs?"

"The landlord was threatening to turn him out."

Carus turned to the Chief Inspector.

"Is that true?"

"That's what he told me."

"Have you arrested him?"

"No. Why?"

"I don't know. A stupid question, now I come to think of it. . . ."

"Do you think he could have killed Sophie?"

The feet, still those feet! It was possible literally to follow the conversation under the table, while all the time Nora's face remained frozen.

"I can't see him killing anybody. What weapon was used? The papers didn't say. The radio didn't mention it either. . . ."

"An automatic."

"But surely Francis never had a gun."

"Indeed he had!" the flat, precise voice of Nora cut in. "You saw it. That night in his place, and you were scared. He had had a lot to drink. He had just described a holdup scene to us. . . .

"He put one of Sophie's stockings over his head and he began threatening us with a gun, telling us to line up against the wall, with our hands in the air. Everyone obeyed, for fun.

"You were the only one who was frightened, and asked if the gun was loaded."

"You're quite right. It all comes back to me. . . . I hadn't thought about it again. I'd had a lot to drink, myself. . . ."

"In the end he put the gun back in the chest of drawers."

"Who was there?" asked Maigret.

"The whole gang. Maki, Dramin, Pochon . . . Dramin was with a girl I had never seen before and about whom I can remember nothing. She was ill and spent an hour in the bathroom."

"Jacques was there too."

"Yes, with his wife, who was already pregnant. . . ."

"Is anybody aware that last year Sophie was almost certainly pregnant as well?"

Why did Nora turn sharply to Carus? The latter looked at her in surprise.

"Did you know?"

"No. If she had a child . . ."

"She didn't have it," the Chief Inspector put in. "She had it aborted between the third and fourth months."

"Then it all went unnoticed."

Maki was coughing, in his corner, as if to call Maigret to order. It was quite a while since he had finished eating and he was becoming impatient.

"We've told you all we know, Inspector.

If you need me, come around and see me in my office."

Did he really wink as he took a visiting card from his wallet and handed it to him?

Maigret had the impression that Carus had lots more to say, but that the presence of Nora was holding him back.

Settled in his corner once again, Maigret filled his pipe while Lapointe remarked, with a slight smile:

"He's still hesitating, but he'll be on his feet in a second."

He was referring to Maki. Unable to look directly into the room, to which his back was turned, the detective had spent his time observing the sculptor, the only person in his field of vision.

"At first, when you were sitting at Carus's table, he was frowning, then he shrugged. He had a carafe of red wine in front of him. Less than five minutes later he had emptied it and signaled to the waiter to bring him another one.

"He didn't miss one of your gestures, or your movements. It was as if he was trying to read everyone's lips. . . .

"Soon he became impatient. At one moment he called the boss over and talked to him in a low voice. The two of them looked in your direction.

"Then he half rose to his feet, after a glance at his watch. I thought he was going to leave, but he ordered an armagnac which was brought to him in a big glass. He's coming over!"

Lapointe was not mistaken. Doubtless annoyed not to see Maigret make a move, Maki had decided to approach him instead. For a moment he stood, towering, between the two men.

"Excuse me," he murmured, putting his hand to his head in a sort of salute. "I wanted to let you know I was just leaving. . . ."

Maigret lit his pipe with a series of little puffs.

"Have a seat, Monsieur Maki. Is that your real name?"

Sitting down heavily, the man grumbled:

"Of course not. It's Lecoeur. . . . Not a name for a sculptor. . . . No one would have taken me seriously."

"Did you know I wanted a word with you?"

"Well, I'm a friend of Francis's too. . . ."

"How did you hear the news?"

"When I got here. I hadn't read the

evening paper, and I never listen to the radio."

"Was it a shock?"

"I'm sorry for Francis. . . ."

"Not for Sophie?"

He was not drunk but his cheeks were flushed, his eyes shining, his gestures exaggerated.

"Sophie was a bitch."

He looked at them in turn as if defying them to deny it.

"What did he—Monsieur Carus—tell you?"

He pronounced the *Monsieur* ironically, as *Mossieu*, clowning it.

"Naturally, he knows nothing. What about you?"

"What do you expect me to know?"

"When did you last see Francis Ricain and his wife?"

"Him, Wednesday. . . ."

"Without her?"

"He was alone."

"What time?"

"Around half past six. He spoke to me before going off to find Bob. . . . I had finished my dinner and was just having my armagnac. . . ."

"What did he say to you?"

119

"He asked me whether I knew where Carus was. I must explain that I, too, work for that gentleman over there. Well, more or less. . . . He needed a clay model for some lousy film, a horror picture, and I knocked something together for him. . . ."

"Did he pay you?"

"Half the agreed-on price. . . . I was waiting for the other half."

"Did Francis tell you why he wanted to see Carus?"

"You know very well. He needed a couple of thousand francs. . . . I hadn't got it. I offered him a drink and he went off. . . ."

"And you haven't seen him since?"

"Neither him nor her. What did that Nora tell you?"

"Not much. . . . She doesn't seem to have a very soft spot for Sophie."

"She never had a soft spot for anybody. . . . Perhaps that's because she's so flat-chested. I beg your pardon. That wasn't very witty. I can't stand the sight of her. Nor him, either, for all his smiles and his handshakes. . . . At first sight they make a very odd couple, he all honey, and she all vinegar, but underneath they're both the same.

"When somebody can be of use to them,

they squeeze him dry, then they chuck him away like an old orange peel. . . ."

"Which is what happened to you?"

"What did they tell you about Francis? You haven't answered me."

"Carus seems to think highly of him."

"And she?"

"She doesn't like him."

"Did they mention Sophie?"

"They told me about what happened in the bedroom one night when everybody had been drinking in the Raphael."

"I was there."

"It seems that nothing happened between Carus and Sophie. . . ."

"My eye!"

"Did you see them?"

"I went into the room twice, to go to the lavatory, and they didn't even notice. She tried once with me, too. She wanted me to model her in the nude—me, an abstract . . . I ended up by giving in to be rid of her."

"Were you her lover?"

"I had to sleep with her, out of courtesy. She would have held it against me if I hadn't done it. I didn't feel very pleased with myself, because of Francis. . . . He didn't deserve to be married to a tramp."

"Did she talk about suicide to you as well?"

"Suicide? She? In the first place, when a woman talks about it, you can be sure she will never do it. She play-acted. With everybody. . . . With a different role for each person."

"Did Francis know?"

Maigret was starting to call him Francis, as well, as if he were gradually becoming intimately acquainted with Ricain.

"If you want my opinion, he suspected it. He shut his eyes to it, but it infuriated him. Did he really love her? . . . There are times when I wonder. . . . He pretended to. He had taken her on and he didn't want to let her go. She must have convinced him that she would kill herself if he left her. . . ."

"Do you think he's talented?"

"More than talented. Of all of us, he's the only one who will do something really important. I'm not bad in my field, but I know my limitations . . . He—well, the day he really gets down to it . . ."

"Thank you, Monsieur Maki."

"Just plain Maki. It's a name that doesn't go with Monsieur. . . ."

"Good night, Maki."

"Good night, Inspector. And this, I presume, is one of your detectives? . . . Good night to you, too."

He went off, with a heavy tread, after a wave to Bob.

Maigret mopped his brow.

"There's only one left: Dramin, with his nose in his script, but I've had enough for tonight."

He looked around for the waiter, asked for the bill. It was Mandille who came running over:

"Allow me to consider both of you as my guests. . . ."

"Impossible," said Maigret with a sigh.

"Will you at least accept a glass of old armagnac?"

They had to go through with it.

"Have you got the information you wanted?"

"I've begun to find my way around the group."

"They aren't all here. And the atmosphere changes from day to day. Some evenings it's very gay, even wild. . . . Haven't you spoken to Gérard?"

He was referring to Dramin, who was heading for the door, script in hand.

"Hey! Gérard . . . Let me introduce Chief

Inspector Maigret and one of his detectives. . . . Will you have a drink with us?"

Very short-sighted, he wore thick glasses and held his head bent forward.

"How do you do? Please excuse me. . . . I have some work to finish. By the way, has Francis been arrested?"

"No. Why?"

"I don't know. Excuse me. . . ."

He unhooked his hat from the hat peg, opened the door, and set off along the sidewalk.

"You mustn't pay any attention to him. He's always like that. I think it's a pose, a way of making himself seem important. . . . He does his absent-minded act, the loner . . . Perhaps he resents it that you didn't go and seek him out. I bet he hasn't read a line all evening. . . ."

"Your good health," murmured Maigret. "For myself, I'll be glad to get to bed. . . ."

Even so, he went by Rue Saint-Charles with Lapointe, and rapped on the studio door. Lourtie opened it. He had taken off his jacket and his hair was disheveled from sleeping in the armchair. The room was lit only by a night light, and the smell of the disinfectant had still not gone.

"Has nobody called?"

"Two reporters. I didn't tell them anything, except to apply to the Quai. . . ."

"No telephone calls?"

"There were a couple."

"Who?"

"I don't know. I heard the phone ring,
I picked it up and said 'Hello'. . . . I heard
breathing at the other end, but the caller
said nothing and soon hung up. . . ."

"Both times?"

"Both times."

"About what time was it?"

"The first time around ten past eight, the
second a few moments ago. . . ."

A few minutes later, Maigret was dozing
in the small black car taking him home.

"I'm exhausted," he confessed to his wife
as he started to undress.

"I hope you had a proper dinner."

"Too much so. . . . I must take you to
that restaurant. It's kept by an old comic-
opera singer who has turned her hand to
cooking. She makes a *chaudrée* such as . . ."

"What time tomorrow?"

"Seven o'clock."

"That early?"

That early; in fact, it was seven o'clock
immediately, with no transition. Maigret
did not even have the sensation of having

been asleep before he could smell coffee and his wife was touching him on the shoulder on her way over to draw back the curtains.

The sun was clear and mild. It was a delight to open the window once you were out of bed and to hear the sparrows chattering.

"I suppose I shouldn't expect you at lunchtime?"

"I probably won't have time to come back to eat. It's a strange case. Strange people. . . . I'm in the movie world, and, as in the movies, everything started with a gag, with the theft of my wallet. . . ."

"Do you think he was the killer?"

Madame Maigret, too, who knew the case only from the newspapers and the radio, was annoyed with herself for having asked the question.

"I'm sorry."

"In any case, it would be hard for me to give you an answer."

"Aren't you going to wear your light coat?"

"No. The weather is the same as yesterday's, and yesterday I wasn't cold. Not even on my way home last night. . . ."

He didn't wait for the bus but hailed a taxi and had himself dropped on the Ile

Saint-Louis. Opposite the Stork there was a *bistrot* surrounded by piles of wood and sacks of coal. Torrence, his face drawn with fatigue, was drinking coffee when the Chief Inspector joined him.

"How did the night go?"

"Like all night watches. Nothing happened, except that I know just when everyone turns out his lights. . . . Someone must be ill on the fourth floor, to the right, because there was light in the window until six o'clock in the morning.

"Your friend Ricain didn't go out. . . . Some of the guests came back. . . . A taxi came for a couple of travelers. . . . A dog attached itself to me and followed me about most of the night. . . . That's about it."

"You can go home and sleep."

"What about my report?"

"You can do it tomorrow."

He went into the hotel, where he had known the proprietor for thirty years. It was a modest establishment which seldom took in anybody but regulars, almost all of them from eastern France, since the owner was from Alsace.

"Is my guest awake?"

"He rang just ten minutes ago to ask for a cup of coffee to be sent up and some croissants. . . . They've just been taken in to him."

"What did he eat last night?"

"Nothing. He must have gone to sleep right away, because when we knocked on his door at about seven o'clock there was no answer. What is he—an important witness? A suspect?"

There was no elevator. Maigret, after climbing the four flights, reached the landing breathing hard, and paused for a moment before knocking at number 43.

"Who is it?"

"Maigret."

"Come in."

Pushing aside the tray on the blanket, Francis emerged from the bed, his thin chest bare, his face covered with a bluish beard, his eyes feverish. He still had a croissant in one hand.

"Excuse my not getting up, but I haven't any pajamas. . . ."

"Did you sleep well?"

"Like a log. I slept so soundly that my head is still heavy. What's the time?"

"A quarter past eight."

The room, small and ill furnished, overlooked the courtyard and the roofs. Voices from the neighboring houses, cries of chil-

128

dren from a school playground, came in through the half-open window.

"Have you found out anything?"

"I had dinner at the Old Wine Press."

Ricain was watching him closely, already on the defensive, and one could sense that he felt the whole world thought he was a liar.

"Were they there?"

"The Caruses were. . . ."

"What did he have to say?"

"He swears you're some kind of genius."

"I presume Nora took the trouble to point out that I'm actually an imbecile?"

"More or less. . . . She certainly likes you less than he does."

"And she liked Sophie even less!"

"Maki was there too."

"Drunk?"

"Only toward the end; then he became a little unsteady."

"He's all right."

"He's sure you will be somebody one day, too."

"Which means that I am nobody. . . ."

He did not finish his croissant. Maigret's arrival seemed to have killed his appetite.

"What do they think happened? That I killed Sophie?"

"To tell the truth, nobody thinks you're guilty. However, some of them imagine that the police think differently, and everyone asked me whether I had arrested you."

"What did you say?"

"The truth."

"That is . . ."

"That you're free."

"Do you really think that's the truth? What am I doing here? You may as well admit it, you had a man on duty all night outside the hotel."

"Did you see him?"

"No, but I know how it goes. . . . And now what are you planning to do with me?"

Maigret was asking himself exactly the same question. He did not want to let Ricain wander freely about Paris, and on the other hand he did not have sufficient grounds to arrest him.

"First of all I am going to ask you to come with me to the Quai des Orfèvres."

"Again?"

"I may have several questions to put to you. Between now and then the frogmen of the River Police may have found your gun."

"What difference does it make whether they find it or not?"

"You have a razor and some soap. There

is a shower at the end of the corridor. I will be waiting for you downstairs, or outside. . . ."

A new day was beginning, as clear, as balmy as the day before and the day before that, but it was too early yet to know what it would bring.

François Ricain made the Chief Inspector very curious, and the opinions he had gathered the day before did nothing to make him less fascinating.

By any standards, he was a youth out of the ordinary, and Carus had been impressed by his possibilities. But then didn't Carus become carried away every time he was confronted with an artist, only to let him drop a few months or a few weeks later?

Maigret resolved to go to see him in his office, to which the producer had given him an enigmatic invitation. He had something to say to him, something he did not want to talk about in front of Nora. She had sensed it, and the Chief Inspector wondered whether Carus would be at Rue de Bassano that morning or whether his mistress would prevent him from going.

So far, he had only touched the periphery of a circle of which there are thousands, tens of thousands, in Paris, composed of friends, relatives, colleagues, lovers and mistresses, regular customers at a café or restaurant, little groups which form, cling together for a while, and disperse to form into other more or less homogeneous little groups.

What was the name of the photographer who had been married twice, had had children by both wives, and had just given another to a new mistress?

He was still confusing the names and the places corresponding to each of them. The fact was, Sophie's murder had been committed by someone intimately acquainted with the household—or with the young woman herself. Otherwise, she would not have opened the door.

Unless someone else had a key?

He was pacing to and fro as Torrence had done all night, but he had the good fortune to be walking in the sun. The street was teeming with housewives who turned around to look at this figure who was walking up and down, hands behind his back, like a schoolmaster supervising a school break.

Yes, he had plenty of questions to put to Francis. And no doubt he was about to be faced once again by a moody creature, in turns bridling and calming down, suspicious, impatient, suddenly giving a roar. . . .

"I'm ready."

Maigret pointed to the *bistrot* with the sacks of coal.

"Do you want a drink?"

"No, thank you."

A shame, since Maigret would have been very pleased to start this spring day with a glass of white wine.

──FIVE────────────────────

IT was a bad stretch to get through. In nearly all of his cases, Maigret came to this period of floating, during which, as his colleagues used to whisper, he appeared to be brooding.

In the first stage—that is to say, when he suddenly found himself face to face with a new world, with people he knew nothing about—it was as if he were breathing in the life around him, mechanically, and filling himself with it like a sponge.

He had done this the day before at the Old Wine Press, his memory registering, as it were subconsciously, the smallest details of the atmosphere, the gestures, the facial quirks of each person.

If he had not felt himself flagging, he would have gone on afterwards to the Zero Club, which some members of the circle frequented.

At the moment he had absorbed a quantity of impressions, a whole jumble of images, of phrases, of words of varying importance, of startled looks, but he did not yet know what to do with them all.

His close acquaintances knew that it was best not to ask him questions nor to question him by looks, as he would quickly become irritable.

As he expected, a note, on his desk, asked him to call Camus, the Magistrate.

"Hello! . . . This is Maigret."

He had seldom worked with this magistrate, whom he classed neither among the outright meddlers nor among those who prudently leave the police time to get on with their work.

"I asked you to phone me because I had a call from the Public Prosecutor's office. . . . He is impatient to know where the inquiry has got to. . . ."

The Chief Inspector almost growled:

"Nowhere."

Which was true. A crime does not pose a mathematical problem. It involves human beings, unknown the day before, who were just passers-by among the rest. And now, all of a sudden, each one of their gestures, their words, takes on weight, and their entire life is gone over with a fine-tooth comb.

"The inquiry is going ahead," he said

instead. "It's likely that we'll have the murder weapon in our hands within an hour or two. The frogmen are scouring the bottom of the Seine for it."

"What have you done with the husband?"

"He's here, in the icebox."

He corrected himself, as that was an expression which could mean something only to the detectives in his unit. When they did not know what to do with a witness, but still wanted to keep him on a string, or when they had a suspect who was not being co-operative, they put him in the "glacière."

They would tell them, as they showed them into the long glass-partitioned waiting room which ran along one side of the corridor:

"Just wait in here a moment, please."

It was always filled with people who were waiting: nervous women, some weeping and dabbing their eyes with their handkerchiefs, would-be tough customers trying to put on a bold front, some honest citizens who waited patiently, staring at the pale green walls, wondering whether their existence had been forgotten.

An hour or two in the glacière was often enough to make people talkative. Witnesses who were determined to say nothing became more amenable.

Sometimes they were "forgotten" for more than half a day, and they would keep watching the door, half rising to their feet every time the attendant came over, hoping it was their turn at last.

They could see the inspectors going off at noon, and would take their courage in both hands to go and ask Joseph:

"Are you sure the Chief Inspector knows that I'm here?"

"He's still in conference."

For want of a better solution, Maigret had put Ricain in the *glacière*.

He translated, for the Magistrate:

"He's in the waiting room. I'll be interrogating him again, as soon as I have more information."

"What is your impression? Guilty?"

Another question which the Magistrate would not have asked if he had worked longer with Maigret.

"I have no impressions."

It was true. He was waiting as long as possible before forming an opinion. And he still had not started "forming." He was keeping his mind free until he had some substantive evidence or until his prisoner broke down.

"Do you think it will be a long business?"

"I hope not."

"Have you discarded the possibility of a simple sordid crime?"

As though all crimes weren't sordid! They didn't speak the same language, they didn't have the same concept of a human being at the Law Courts as they did at Police Headquarters.

It was difficult to believe that an unknown man, looking for money, would have presented himself at Rue Saint-Charles after ten o'clock at night, and that Sophie Ricain, already in her nightgown, would have let him into the studio without being suspicious.

Either her killer had a key, or else it was somebody she knew and trusted. Especially if the murderer had had to open the drawer in the chest in her presence and take out the gun.

"Kindly keep me informed. Don't leave me too long without news. The Prosecutor's office is getting impatient."

All right! The Prosecutor's office a always impatient. Gentlemen who live comfortably in their offices and who see crime only in terms of legal texts and statistics. A telephone call from the Ministry makes them tremble in their shoes.

"Why has nobody been arrested yet?"

The Prosecutor himself was under pressure from the newspapers. A good crime is good business for them, particularly if it presents a spectacular new angle every day. If the reader is kept in ignorance too long, he forgets about the case. And some nice front-page headlines are gone to waste.

"Certainly, Judge. . . . Yes, Judge. . . . I'll be calling you, Judge. . . ."

He winked at Janvier.

"Go and take an occasional look in the waiting room to see how he's reacting. He's the kind that'll either have a nervous breakdown or come and beat on my door."

In spite of it all he went through his mail and attended the morning conference, where he saw his colleagues and where they discussed unemotionally several of the current cases.

"Anything new, Maigret?"

"Nothing new, Director."

Here, they did not insist. You were among professionals.

When the Chief Inspector returned to his

office, just before ten o'clock, the River Police were asking for him.

"Did you find the weapon?"

"Fortunately, the current has not been strong these days and the Seine was dragged at this point last autumn. My men found the weapon almost immediately, at about ten yards from the left bank, a 6.35 Belgian-made automatic. There were still five bullets left."

"Send it around to Gastinne-Renette, will you?"

And, to Janvier:

"Take care of it, will you—he's got the bullet already."

"Right, Chief."

Maigret was on the point of calling up Rue de Bassano, decided not to announce himself, and set off for the main staircase, taking care not to look toward the waiting room.

His departure could not have escaped the notice of Ricain, who must have wondered where he was going. He ran into Lapointe on his way out and instead of taking a taxi, as he had intended, he had himself driven to the building where Carus had his offices.

He paused to read the copper nameplates

in the entrance arch, noting that there was a movie company on almost every floor. The company he was concerned with was called Carrossoc, and its reception rooms were on the first floor.

"Shall I come with you?"

"I'd rather you did."

Not only was it his way of doing things, but it was recommended in the manual of instructions for officers of the Police Department.

They entered a somewhat dark hall, with a single window overlooking the courtyard, where a chauffeur could be seen polishing a Rolls-Royce. A red-headed secretary was at the switchboard.

"Monsieur Carus, please."

"I don't know if he's in."

As if he did not have to pass her to reach the other offices!

"Whom shall I announce? Do you have an appointment?"

"Chief Inspector Maigret."

She got up, endeavoring to lead them to the anteroom, to put them, in their turn, in the *glacière*.

"Thank you. We'll wait here. . . ."

She was obviously not pleased. Instead of calling her boss, she disappeared through a padded door and was gone for three or four minutes.

She was not the first person to come back. Instead, it was Carus himself, in light gray worsted, freshly shaved and exuding a smell of lavender.

Evidently he had just come from his barber, and no doubt he had had a face massage. He was just the type to take his ease every morning for a good half hour in the reclining chair.

"How are you, my friend?"

He held out a cordial hand to the good friend he had not even known at six o'clock the previous evening.

"Come right in, please. You too, young man. . . . I presume this is one of your colleagues?"

"Inspector Lapointe."

"You may leave us, Mademoiselle. . . . I'm not in to anybody and I won't take any calls, except from New York."

He explained, with a smile:

"I hate to be interrupted by the telephone. . . ."

There were nonetheless three of them on his desk. The room was enormous, the walls decorated with beige leather to match the armchairs, the thick pile carpet a very soft chestnut color.

As for the immense Brazilian rosewood desk, it was piled high with enough files to keep a dozen secretaries busy.

"Sit down, please. What may I offer you?"

He went over to a low piece of furniture which proved to be a sizable bar.

"It's a little early for an apéritif, perhaps, but I happened to notice that you are a connoisseur of beer. . . . So am I. I have some excellent beer, which I have sent directly from Munich. . . ."

He was being even more expansive than the day before, perhaps because he did not have to bother about Nora's reactions.

"Yesterday, you caught me off base. . . . I was not expecting to meet you. I had had two or three whiskies before I got to the restaurant, and what with the champagne . . . I wasn't drunk. I never am. Even so, I have only a rather dim recollection this morning of certain details of our conversation. My wife reproached me for talking too much and too enthusiastically. . . . Your good health! I hope that's not the impression I gave you?"

"You seem to consider François Ricain somebody worthwhile, with every chance

of becoming one of our leading movie directors. . . ."

"I must have said that, yes. . . . It's in
my nature to be open to young people, and
I'm easily carried away. . . ."

"You are no longer of the same opinion?"

"Oh, of course, of course! But with certain qualifications. I find a tendency, in
this young man, toward disorder, toward
anarchy. At one moment he will show too
much self-confidence, and at the next he
has none at all. . . ."

"If I remember your words correctly,
in your opinion they were a very devoted
couple."

Carus had settled down in one of the
armchairs with his legs crossed, glass in one
hand, cigar in the other.

"Did I say that?"

Suddenly changing his mind, he sprang
to his feet, put the glass down on a console table, took several puffs at his cigar,
and started pacing the carpet.

"Listen, Inspector, I was hoping you
would come around this morning. . . ."

"So I gathered."

"Nora is an exceptional woman. Although
she never so much as sets foot in my offices,

I could describe her as the best business associate I have. . . ."

"You mentioned her gifts as a . . . medium."

He waved a hand as if to erase words written on an invisible blackboard.

"That's what I say in her presence, because it pleases her. . . . The truth is that she's got solid common sense and is seldom wrong in her appraisal of people. Personally, I get carried away. . . . I trust people too easily."

"She's a sort of safety catch?"

"Something like it. . . . I've made up my mind quite definitely to marry her, when my divorce has gone through. It's already as if . . ."

He was obviously getting into difficulties, searching for words, while his eyes remained fixed on the ash of his cigar.

"Well . . . How can I put it? Although Nora's a superior woman, she still can't help being jealous. That's why yesterday, in her presence, I was obliged to lie to you. . . ."

"The bedroom incident?"

"Precisely. It didn't happen as I recounted it, of course. It is true that Sophie ran away to the bedroom to cry after Nora had said a lot of mean things to her. I don't remember exactly what they were, as we had all been drinking. In short, I went to comfort her. . . ."

"Was she your mistress?"

"If you insist on the word. . . . She flung herself into my arms, one thing led to another, and we were careless, very careless. . . ."

"And your wife caught you at it?"

"A Chief Inspector would not have hesitated to corroborate a charge of adultery. . . ."

He smiled, with a touch of satisfaction.

"Tell me, Monsieur Carus. I presume pretty girls must pass through your offices every day. Most of them are ready to do anything to land a part."

"That's correct."

"I believe I am right in thinking that you have been known to take advantage of this circumstance."

"I make no secret of it. . . ."

"Even from Nora?"

"Let me explain. . . . If I take advantage, as you put it, of a pretty girl now and then, Nora doesn't let it upset her too much on condition that there is no future. . . . It's part of the job. All men do the same, unless

146

they don't have the opportunity. Even you yourself, Chief Inspector . . ."

Maigret looked at him stonily, unsmiling.

"Excuse me, if I have shocked you. . . . Where was I? . . . I am not unaware that you have questioned some of my friends and that you will continue to do so. I prefer to be quite straight with you. You have heard the way Nora talks about Sophie. . . .

"I would rather you didn't form an impression of the girl from what she said . . .

"She wasn't ambitious, quite the contrary, and she wasn't the girl to sleep with just anybody. . . .

"She had been drawn to Ricain on an impulse when she was still a kid, and it was bound to happen, he has a kind of magnetism. . . . Women are impressed by men who are tortured, ambitious, bitter, violent. . . ."

"Is that your picture of him?"

"What about you?"

"I don't know yet."

"In short, he married her. She put her trust in him. . . . She followed him about like a well-trained little dog, keeping her mouth shut when he didn't want her to talk, taking up as little space as possible so as not to get in his way, and accepting the precarious life he led."

"Was she unhappy?"

"She suffered, but she took care to hide it. . . . Well, he needed her, her passive presence, but there were moments when he became irritated with her, complaining that she was a dead weight, an obstacle to his career, accusing her of being a dumb animal. . . ."

"Did she tell you this?"

"I had already guessed it, from remarks made in my presence. . . ."

"Did you become her confidant?"

"If you want to put it that way. . . . In spite of myself, I assure you. She felt herself lost in a world too harsh for her, and she had nobody to turn to. . . ."

"At what period did you become her lover?"

"Another word I dislike. . . . It was mostly pity, tenderness which I felt for her. My intention was to help her. . . ."

"To have a career in the movies?"

"I'm going to surprise you, but it was my idea and she resisted it. . . . She was not a striking beauty, one of those traffic-stoppers like Nora. . . .

"I have a pretty good instinct for the

148

public's tastes. If I hadn't, I wouldn't be doing the job I do. With her somewhat ordinary face, and her small, rather fragile body, Sophie was exactly the picture of the young girl as most people imagine her to be.

"Parents would have seen their daughter in her, young people their cousin or their girl friend. . . . Do you see what I mean?"

"Did you have plans to launch her?"

"Let's say I was thinking about it. . . ."

"Did you tell her?"

"Not in so many words. I sounded her out discreetly. . . ."

"Where did your meetings take place?"

"That is an unpleasant question, but I am obliged to answer it, am I not?"

"Especially since I would find out for myself."

"Well, I've rented a furnished studio, quite chic, quite comfortable, in a new apartment house in Rue François-Premier. To be exact, it's the big one on the corner of Avenue Georges V. I only have three hundred yards to walk from here. . . ."

"One second. This studio—was it intended exclusively for your rendezvous with Sophie, or was it for others as well?"

"In theory it was for Sophie. . . . It was

difficult for us to have any privacy here, and I couldn't go to her house either. . . ."

"You never went there when her husband was away?"

"Once or twice. . . ."

"Recently?"

"The last time was a fortnight ago. She hadn't telephoned me as she usually did. I didn't see her in Rue François-Premier either. I called her at home and she told me she wasn't feeling well. . . ."

"Was she ill?"

"Depressed. Francis was becoming more and more irritable. . . . Sometimes he was even violent. . . . She was at the end of her tether and wanted to go away, anywhere, work as a salesgirl in the first store she came across. . . ."

"Did you not advise her to do anything?"

"I gave her the address of one of my lawyers to consult about the possibility of a divorce. It would have been better for both of them. . . ."

"Had she made up her mind?"

"She was hesitating. She felt sorry for Francis. She felt it her duty to stay with him, until he achieved some success. . . ."

"Did she talk to him about it?"

"Certainly not. . . ."

"How can you be so sure?"

"Because he would have reacted violently. . . ."

"I would like to ask you a question, Monsieur Carus. Think carefully before answering, because I won't hide from you the fact that it is important. You knew that, about a year ago, Sophie was pregnant?"

He flushed scarlet all of a sudden, nervously stubbed out his cigar in the glass ashtray.

"Yes, I knew," he muttered, sitting down again. "But I can tell you right away, I can swear by all that's dear to me in this world, that the child was not mine. . . . I noticed that she was upset, preoccupied. I mentioned it to her. She admitted that she was expecting a child and that Francis would be furious. . . ."

"Why?"

"Because it would be another burden, another obstacle to his career. He was on the dole. With a child . . . In short, she was sure he would never forgive her, and she asked me for the address of a midwife or an obliging doctor. . . ."

"Did you help her?"

"I have to admit that I transgressed the law."

"It's a bit late now to pretend anything else."

"I did her that small service. . . ."

"Francis knew nothing about it?"

"No. He's too wrapped up in himself to notice what is going on around him, even when it concerns his wife. . . ."

He rose hesitantly and, no doubt to restore his composure, went to fetch some fresh bottles from the bar.

Everyone called him Monsieur Gaston, with a respectful familiarity, for he was a conscientious and worthy man, aware of the weighty responsibilities of the concierge of a great hotel. He had spotted Maigret before he had even entered the revolving doors, and had puckered his brows while he quickly passed in mental review the faces of the hotel guests who might have caused this visit from the police.

"Wait here for me a moment, Lapointe."

He had to wait, himself, for an old lady to check the time of arrival of an airplane from Buenos Aires before discreetly shaking Monsieur Gaston's hand.

"Don't worry. Nothing unpleasant."

"When I see you coming, I can't help wondering. . . ."

"If I am not mistaken, Monsieur Carus has a suite here, on the fourth floor?"

"That's right. With Madame Carus. . . ."

"Is she registered in that name?"

"Well, it's what we call her here. . . ."

The shadow of a smile sufficed to make Monsieur Gaston's meaning clear.

"Is she upstairs?"

He glanced at the key board.

"I don't know why I look. A habit . . . At this hour she'll certainly be having her breakfast. . . ."

"Monsieur Carus has been away this week, hasn't he?"

"Wednesday and Thursday. . . ."

"Did he go alone?"

"His chauffeur took him to Orly around five o'clock. . . . I think he had to take the Frankfurt plane."

"When did he come back?"

"Yesterday afternoon, from London."

"Although you aren't here at night yourself, perhaps you have a way of finding out if Madame Carus went out on Wednesday evening and at what time she came home?"

"That's easy. . . ."

He leafed through the pages of a big register bound in black.

"When they come home in the evening, the guests usually stop for a moment to tell my colleague on the night shift what time they want to be called and what they will have for breakfast.

"Madame Carus never fails. We don't note the time they come in, but it's possible to fix an approximate time by the order in which the names are listed on the page.

"Wait now. There are only a dozen names for Wednesday, before hers. . . . Miss Trevor . . . An early bedder, an old lady who always comes home before ten o'clock. The Maxwells . . . At first glance, I would say she came back before midnight, say between ten o'clock and midnight. At any rate, before the theaters were out. I'll ask the night porter to confirm it. . . ."

"Thank you. Would you announce me?"

"Do you want to see her? Do you know her?"

"I had coffee last evening with her and her husband. Let's say it's a courtesy visit."

"Put me through to 403, please. . . . Hello? . . . Madame Carus? . . . This is the concierge. . . . Chief Inspector Maigret is asking if he may come up. . . . Yes. . . . Right. . . . I'll tell him. . . ."

And, to Maigret:

"She wants you to wait ten minutes."

Was it to finish that fearful and elaborate ritual of making herself up, or was it to telephone Rue de Bassano?

The Chief Inspector went back to Lapointe, and the two of them wandered in silence from showcase to showcase, admiring the stones exhibited by the leading Parisian jewelers, as well as the fur coats and the linens.

"Are you thirsty?"

"No, thank you."

They had the unpleasant sensation of attracting attention, and it was a relief when the ten minutes were up and they went into one of the elevators.

"Fourth floor."

Nora, who herself let them in, was wearing a pale green satin dressing gown that matched her eyes, and her hair seemed more bleached than the day before, almost white.

The sitting room was enormous, with light coming in from two bay windows, one of which opened onto a balcony.

"I wasn't expecting your visit, and you caught me as I was getting up. . . ."

"I hope we are not interrupting your breakfast?"

The tray was not in the room, but was probably next door.

"It's not my husband you want to see? . . . He left for the office quite some time ago. . . ."

"I was passing by, and I wanted to ask you a few questions. Of course, there's no obligation to answer. First of all, a question I am putting, as a matter of routine, to everybody who knew Sophie Ricain. Don't read anything into it. Where were you on Wednesday night?"

Without flinching, she sat down in a white armchair and asked:

"At what time?"

"Where did you have dinner?"

"Just a moment. Wednesday? . . . Yesterday, you were with us. . . . On Thursday I dined alone at Fouquet's, not in the first-floor dining room, which is where I go when I'm with Carus, but on the ground floor, at a small table. . . . Wednesday . . . On Wednesday, I didn't have dinner, that's all there is to it. . . .

"I should tell you that except for a light breakfast I usually only have one other meal a day. If I have lunch, I don't dine. . . . So, if I dine it's because I didn't have lunch. On Wednesday we lunched at the Berkeley with friends. . . .

"In the afternoon I had a fitting, just

156

around the corner from here. . . . Then I had a drink at Jean's, in Rue Marboeuf. . . . I must have come home around nine o'clock."

"Did you go straight up to your suite?"

"That's right. I read until one o'clock in the morning, as I can't get to sleep early. . . . Before that I watched television. . . ."

There was a set in a corner of the room.

"Don't ask me what program it was. All I know is that there were young singers, boys and girls. . . . Do you want me to call the floor waiter? . . . True, it's not the same. . . . But tonight you can question the night waiter. . . ."

"Did you order anything?"

"A champagne split. . . ."

"At what time?"

"I don't know. . . . Shortly before getting ready for bed. . . . Do you suspect me of going to Rue Saint-Charles and murdering that wretched Sophie?"

"I don't suspect anybody. I am only doing my duty, and in the process trying to be as unobtrusive as possible. Last evening you referred to Sophie Ricain in terms which implied a lack of warmth between the two of you."

"I made no effort to hide it. . . ."

"There was talk of an evening here, when you found her in your husband's arms. . . ."

"I oughtn't to have brought it up. . . . It was just to show you that she would throw herself at any man who came along, and that she wasn't the little white lamb or the timid little slave that certain people have doubtless described. . . ."

"Of whom are you thinking?"

"I don't know. . . . Men tend to let themselves be taken in by that sort of act. Most of the people we mix with probably take me for a cold, ambitious, calculating woman. Go on, admit it!"

"Nobody has spoken to me in such terms."

"I'm sure that's what they think. . . . Even a person like Bob, who ought to know better . . . Little Sophie, on the other hand, all sweet and submissive, is the misunderstood girl everybody is sorry for. . . . You can think what you like. . . . I'm telling you the truth."

"Was Carus her lover?"

"Who says so?"

"You told me yourself that you had surprised them . . ."

"I said she had thrown herself into his arms, that she was sniveling to get sympathy, but I never said Carus was her lover. . . ."

"All the others were, weren't they? Isn't that what I'm meant to understand?"

"Ask them. We'll see if they dare to deny it. . . ."

"And Ricain?"

"You put me in an awkward position. . . . It's not up to me to pass final judgment on people we mix with and who are not necessarily friends. Did I say Francis knew what was going on? It's possible. . . . I don't remember. . . . I get carried away.

"Carus was flattered by the boy, and insisted that he had a fantastic future before him. . . . Personally, I regard him as a little sponger posing as an artist. . . . You can take your pick."

Maigret rose, pulling his pipe from his pocket.

"That's all I wanted to ask you. Ah! Just one small question. Sophie had become pregnant, a year ago now."

"I know. . . ."

"Did she tell you about it?"

"She was two or three months pregnant, I forget which. Francis didn't want a child, because of his career. . . . So she asked me if I knew an address . . . She had heard about Switzerland, but was hesitating to make the journey. . . ."

"Were you able to help her?"

"I told her I knew no one. . . . I was not keen for Carus and myself to become involved in that sort of thing. . . ."

"How did it end?"

"Well, no doubt, from her point of view, since she made no further mention of it and she didn't have a child. . . ."

"Thank you."

"Have you been to Carus's office?"

Maigret answered the question with another:

"Hasn't he telephoned?"

He was making sure, in this way, that once she was by herself the young woman would ring Rue de Bassano.

"Thank you, Gaston," he said, as he passed the concierge.

Out on the sidewalk he took a deep breath.

"If it ends up with a general confrontation of witnesses, it should be quite an exciting event."

As though to wash out his mouth, he went and drank a glass of white wine in the first bar he passed. He had been wanting one all morning, ever since the events of

Rue Saint-Louis-en-L'Ile, and Carus's beer had not removed the urge.

"To the Quai, Lapointe, young man. I'm curious to see what sort of state our Francis is in."

He was not in the *glacière*, which contained only an old lady together with a very young man with a broken nose. In his office he found Janvier, who gestured toward Ricain, fuming in a chair.

"I had to let him in here, Chief. He was making such a racket in the corridor, demanding to see the Director, threatening to tell all the newspapers. . . ."

"I'm within my right. . . . !" stormed the youth. "I've had enough of being treated like an imbecile or a criminal. . . . My wife has been killed and it's I who am being watched, as if I were trying to escape. I'm not left one moment's peace, and . . ."

"Do you want a lawyer?"

Francis looked him in the eyes, hesitantly, his pupils dilated with hatred.

"You . . . you . . ."

His anger was preventing him from finding words.

"You give yourself fatherly airs. You must love yourself for being so kind, so patient, so understanding. . . . I thought

161

that way too. . . . Now I see that everything they say about you is just hot air."

He was becoming carried away, his words tumbling on top of one another, his speech getting faster and faster.

"How much do you pay them, the newspapermen, to flatter you? What a damn fool I was. When I saw your name in the wallet I thought I was saved, that at last I had found someone who would understand.

"I called you. . . . For without my telephone call you wouldn't have found me. With your money, I'd have been able . . . When I think I didn't even take the price of a meal. . . .

"And what's the result? You shut me up in a crummy hotel bedroom. With a detective standing guard on the sidewalk. . . .

"Then you put me into your rat trap and every now and then your men come and take a peek at me through the glass. . . . I totted up at least twelve who gave themselves this little treat. . . ."

"All this, because my wife was killed in my absence and the police are powerless to protect citizens. Because the next thing is, instead of looking for the real culprit, they have to seize on the obvious suspect, the husband who was unfortunate enough to take fright. . . ."

Maigret was puffing slowly at his pipe, facing Francis, in full spate now, standing in the middle of the room waving his clenched fists.

"Have you finished?"

He put the question in a calm voice, without any trace of impatience or irony.

"Do you still want to call a lawyer?"

"I am quite capable of defending myself. And when the time comes and you realize your mistake and let me go, you'll have to . . ."

"You're free to go."

"What do you mean?"

His fury abated all of a sudden, and he stood there, his arms dangling, staring in disbelief at the Chief Inspector.

"You've been free all along, as you know perfectly well. If I provided you with a roof over your head last night it's because you had no money and you did not, or so I presume, want to sleep in the studio in Rue Saint-Charles."

Maigret had pulled his wallet from his pocket, the same wallet that Francis had stolen from him on the platform of the bus. He took out two ten-franc notes.

"Here is something to buy a snack and get you back to Rue de Grenelle. One of your friends will lend you a little money to tide you over. I should inform you that I have had a telegram sent to your wife's parents in Concarneau, and that her father arrives in Paris at six o'clock this evening. I don't know whether he will get in touch with you. I didn't speak to him on the telephone myself, but it seems he wants to take his daughter's body back to Brittany."

Ricain no longer spoke of leaving. He was trying to understand.

"Of course, you're the husband, and it's up to you to decide."

"What do you advise me to do?"

"Funerals are expensive. I don't suppose you will often have time to visit the cemetery. So if the family are very anxious . . ."

"I'll have to think about it. . . ."

Maigret had opened the door of his cupboard, where he always kept a bottle of brandy and some glasses, a precaution which had often proved useful.

He filled a single glass, and offered it to the young man.

"Drink that."

"What about you?"

"No thank you."

Francis drank the brandy down in one gulp.

"Why are you giving me liquor?"

"To steady you."

"I suppose I'll be followed?"

"Not even that. On condition you let me know where I can get in touch with you. Are you planning to return to Rue Saint-Charles?"

"Where else could I go?"

"One of my Inspectors is there at the moment. By the way, last evening the telephone rang twice in the studio. The Inspector picked up the receiver and both times nobody answered."

"It couldn't have been I, because . . ."

"I'm not asking if it was you. Somebody called the studio. Somebody who had not read the newspapers. What I am wondering is whether that man or that woman was expecting to hear your voice or your wife's."

"I have no idea. . . ."

"Hasn't it ever happened that you have picked up the receiver and only heard breathing?"

"What are you driving at?"

"Suppose they thought you were out, and wanted to talk to Sophie?"

"That again? What have they been telling you, all the people you were questioning last evening and this morning? What scraps of scandal are you trying to . . . to . . ."

"One question, Francis."

The latter started, surprised to hear himself addressed in this way.

"What did you do, about a year and a half ago, when you found out that Sophie was pregnant?"

"She's never been pregnant."

"Has the medical report arrived, Janvier?"

"Here it is, Chief. Delaplanque has just sent it through."

Maigret ran his eye over it.

"There! You can see for yourself that I'm not making false allegations, and that I am simply referring to medical facts."

Ricain was looking savagely at him once more.

"And what's all this about, for God's sake? Anyone would think you had sworn to drive me out of my mind. First you accuse me of killing my wife, then . . ."

"I have never accused you."

"It's just as if . . . You insinuate . . . Then, to calm me down . . ."

He seized the glass which had contained

the brandy, and dashed it violently to the floor.

"I ought to get to know your tricks better! What a fine movie that would make! But the Ministry would take care to stop it. . . . So, Sophie was pregnant a year ago? And, of course, as we had no children, I presume we took ourselves to an abortionist. Is that right? So that's the new charge that's been dreamed up for me, because you couldn't make the other one stick!"

"I never pretended you were aware of what was happening. I asked if your wife mentioned it to you. In fact she went to someone else."

"Because it had to do with someone besides me, the husband?"

"She wanted to spare you the worry, perhaps a battle with your conscience. She imagined a child would be a handicap at this point in your career."

"And so?"

"She confided in one of your friends."

"But who, for God's sake?"

"Carus."

"What? You want me to believe that Carus . . ."

"He told me so this morning. Nora confirmed it half an hour later, with just one variation. According to her, Sophie was not alone when she spoke of being a mother. You were both there."

"She was lying. . . ."

"Quite possibly."

"Do you believe her?"

"For the time being, I believe nobody."

"Me included."

"You included, Francis. But even so, you're free to go."

Maigret lit his pipe, sat at his desk, and began thumbing through some papers.

──SIX──

RICAIN had left hesitantly, awkwardly, suspicious like a bird that sees its cage open, and Janvier had shot an inquiring glance at his Chief. Was he really being let loose, without any kind of tail being put on him?

Pretending not to understand the mute question, Maigret went on thumbing through his papers, finally got up and went and stood at the window.

He was morose. Janvier had returned to the Inspectors' room and was exchanging views in an undertone with Lapointe when the Chief Inspector came in. Instinctively the two men separated, but it made no difference. Maigret seemed not to have seen them.

He was pacing back and forth between offices as if he did not know what to do with his heavy body, pausing by a typewriter, a telephone, or an empty chair, shuffling papers for no particular reason.

Finally he grumbled:

"Tell my wife I won't be home for dinner."

He didn't call her himself, which was significant. Nobody dared to speak to him, far less ask questions. In the Inspectors' room, everybody was in a state of suspense. He sensed it, and with a shrug he returned to his office and picked up his hat.

He said nothing, neither where he was going nor when he would be back, left no instructions, as if all of a sudden he had lost interest in the case.

On the big dusty staircase he emptied his pipe, tapping it against his heel, then crossed the courtyard and nodded vaguely in the direction of the porter, and set off toward Place Dauphine.

Perhaps it was not really where he wanted to go. His mind was elsewhere, in an area which was not familiar to him, Boulevard de Grenelle, Rue Saint-Charles, Avenue de La-Motte-Picquet.

He could see the dark outline of the elevated, which cut a diagonal in the sky, thought he could hear the muted rumble of carriages. . . . The padded, somewhat syrupy atmosphere of the Old Wine Press, the liveliness of Rose, who never stopped wiping her hands on her apron, the waxlike

170

face of the former stunt man, with its ironical smile . . .

Maki, huge and gentle in his corner, his eye growing darker and more bleary as he drank . . . Gérard Dramin, with his ascetic face, ceaselessly correcting his script . . . Carus, who took so much trouble to be friendly with everyone, and Nora, artificial from dyed hair to fingertips . . .

One would have said his feet were carrying him, without his knowledge, by force of habit, to the Dauphine, and he greeted the proprietor, sniffed the restaurant's warm smell, and went over to his corner, where he had sat on the bench thousands of times before.

"There's *andouillette*, Inspector."

"With mashed potatoes?"

"And to start with?"

"Anything. A carafe of Sancerre."

His colleague from Records was eating in another corner with someone from the Ministry of the Interior whom Maigret knew only by sight. The other customers were nearly all regulars, lawyers who would get through their meals quickly and then go across the square to plead their cases, a magistrate, a Gaming Act Inspector.

The proprietor, too, realized that this was

not the moment to start a conversation, and Maigret ate slowly, with concentration, as if it were an important act.

Half an hour later he was walking around the Law Courts, his hands behind his back, slowly, like a lonely man exercising his dog, then he was back once more on the great staircase, and finally pushing open his office door.

A note from Gastinne-Renette was waiting for him. It was not the final report. The gun found in the Seine was indeed the one which had fired the bullet in Rue Saint-Charles.

He shrugged his shoulders again, for he had known it all along. At moments he felt himself submerged under these secondary questions, these reports, these telephone calls, these routine activities.

Joseph, the ancient attendant, knocked on his door and as usual came in without waiting for an answer.

"There's a gentleman to see you. . . ."

Maigret put out a hand, glanced at the form:

"Show him in."

The man was in black, which emphasized his ruddy complexion and the shock of gray hair on his head.

"Sit down, Monsieur Le Gal. Let me offer my condolences. . . ."

The man had had time for weeping on the train, and it seemed that he had had a few drinks to give himself courage. His eyes were hazy, and his words came with difficulty.

"What have they done with her . . . ? I didn't want to go to her place, in case I should meet that man, for I think I would strangle him with my bare hands. . . ."

How many times had Maigret witnessed this same reaction from families?

"In any case, Monsieur Le Gal, the body is no longer in Rue Saint-Charles. It's in the Police Pathological Department. . . ."

"Where's that?"

"Near Austerlitz bridge, on the river. I'll have you driven over, because you must make an official identification of your daughter."

"Did she suffer?"

He was clenching his fists, but it was not a convincing gesture. It was as though his impetus had evaporated on the way, together with his rage, so that he was merely repeating words he no longer believed in.

"I hope you have arrested him?"

"There is no proof against her husband."

"But, Inspector, from the day she first spoke to me about this man, I predicted it would all end badly. . . ."

"Did she take him to see you?"

"I never saw him. I only know him from a bad photograph. She didn't want to introduce him to us. . . . From the moment she met him the family no longer meant anything to her. . . .

"All she wanted was to get married as quickly as possible. She had even drawn up the letter of consent, which I had to sign. . . . Her mother wanted to stop me. In the end I gave in, so now I hold myself partly responsible for what happened. . . ."

Wasn't there always this side of things in every case, at once sordid and moving?

"Was she your only child?"

"Fortunately, we have a son of fifteen."

Actually, Sophie had vanished from their lives a long time before.

"Could I take the body back to Concarneau?"

"As far as we are concerned the formalities have been completed."

He had said "formalities."

"You mean they've . . . I mean, there was a . . ."

"A post-mortem, yes. As for transportation, I advise you to get in touch with an undertaker's who will see to the arrangements."

"And him?"

"I've spoken to him. He has no objection to her being buried in Concarneau."

"I hope he isn't thinking of coming? Because if he does, I won't be answerable for what happens. There are people in our part of the world who have less self-control than I have. . . ."

"I know. I'll see to it that he stays in Paris."

"It's he, isn't it?"

"I assure you I do not know."

"Who else would have killed her? She only saw through his eyes. He had literally hypnotized her. Since her marriage she hasn't written three times, and she didn't even take the trouble to send us a New Year card. . . .

"I found out her new address through the newspapers. I thought she was still in the little hotel in Montmartre where they lived after their marriage. A funny sort of wedding, with no relatives, no friends! . . . Do *you* think that's a promising start?"

Maigret heard him out, nodding sympathetically, then closed the door behind his visitor, whose breath reeked of alcohol.

And Ricain's father? Wouldn't he, too, be making an appearance? The Chief Inspector was expecting him. He had sent one detective to Orly, another to the Raphael to photograph the page in the registry which the concierge had shown him.

"There are two reporters, Chief Inspector. . . ."

"Turn them over to Janvier."

Janvier came in a moment later.

"What do I tell them?"

"Anything. That we're coming along with our inquiries."

"They thought they would find Ricain here, and they brought a photographer along with them."

"Let them look. Let them go and knock on the Rue Saint-Charles door if they like."

He was laboriously following a train of thought, or rather several trains of contradictory thoughts. Had he been right to let Francis go, in the overwrought state he was in?

He would not get far with the twenty francs the Chief Inspector had given him. He would be forced to start his begging rounds again, knocking on doors, calling on friends.

"Well, it's not my fault if . . ."

Anybody would have thought Maigret had an uneasy conscience, that he had something with which to reproach himself. He kept returning to the starting point of the affair, the very beginning: the platform of the bus.

He could see in his mind's eye the woman with the blank face whose shopping bag bumped against his legs. A chicken, some butter, eggs, leeks, some leafy celery. He had wondered why she was doing her shopping so far afield.

A young man was smoking a pipe that was too short and too heavy. His fair hair was as pale as Nora's dyed hair.

At the time, he still had not met Carus's mistress, who passed herself off, at the Raphael and elsewhere, as his wife.

For a moment he had lost his balance and somebody had neatly extracted his wallet from his pocket.

Somehow he would have liked to dissect that instant of time, which seemed to him to be the most important one of all. The unknown man leaving the moving bus, in Rue du Temple, and hurrying away, zigzagging among the housewives, toward the narrow streets of the Marais . . .

His face was clear in the Chief Inspector's memory. He had been certain he would recognize him, because the thief had turned around. . . .

Why had he turned around? And why, on discovering Maigret's identity from the contents of the wallet, had he put it in a brown envelope and sent it back?

At the time, the time of the theft, he thought he was being followed. He was convinced that he would be accused of his wife's murder and that they would come and shut him up. He had given a curious reason for not wanting to let himself be arrested. Claustrophobia . . .

It was the first time, in the thirty years of his career, that he had heard a suspect give this as a reason for flight. On reflection, however, Maigret was forced to concede that sometimes it was perhaps the case. He did not take the subway himself, except when there was no other means of transportation, because he felt suffocated in it.

And here in his office, what about this compulsive jumping to his feet every few seconds and standing by the window?

Sometimes people, especially people from

the Prosecutor's office, criticized him for doing the Inspectors' work for them, for going and interrogating witnesses on the spot instead of summoning them, for returning to the scene of a crime without any concrete reason, even for taking over watches himself, in sunshine and rain alike.

He liked his office, but he could never stay there for two hours at a stretch without feeling an urge to escape. When a case was on he would have liked to be everywhere at the same time.

Bob Mandille must be having his siesta now, for the Old Wine Press shut late at night. Did Rose take a siesta too? What would she have told him if they had sat down together at a table in the deserted restaurant?

They all had different opinions about Ricain and Sophie. Some of them, like Carus, did not mind changing their opinions and contradicting themselves after a lapse of a few hours.

Who was Sophie? One of those teenagers who throw themselves at every man they meet? An ambitious girl who had believed that Francis would launch her on a film star's career?

She used to meet the producer in a hideaway in Rue François-Premier. That is, if Carus was telling the truth.

They had talked about Ricain's jealousy, and how he virtually never left his wife. On the other hand, he did not hesitate to borrow money from her lover.

Did he know? Did he close his eyes?

"Show him in. . . ."

He had expected it. It was the father. Ricain's, this time, a large, powerful man, with a youthful look despite his iron-gray hair, which he wore in a crewcut.

"I hesitated to come. . . ."

"Sit down, Monsieur Ricain."

"Is he here?"

"No. He was this morning, but he's gone."

The man had strongly etched features, pale eyes, a thoughtful expression.

"I would have come earlier, but I was on duty as engineer on the Ventimiglia-Paris . . ."

"When did you last see Francis?"

Surprised, he echoed:

"Francis?"

"That's what most of his friends call him."

"At home we called him François. Wait now. . . . He came to see me just before Christmas. . . ."

180

"Had you remained on good terms?"

"I saw very little of him."

"And his wife?"

"He introduced her to me a few days before the marriage."

"How old was he when his mother died?"

"Fifteen. . . . He was a good boy, but he was already beginning to be difficult and he couldn't stand being corrected. . . . It was no use trying to stop him from doing what he wanted. . . . I wanted him to join the railway . . . Not necessarily as a worker. . . . He would have got a good desk job. . . ."

"Why did he go and see you before Christmas?"

"To ask for money, of course. . . . He never came for anything else. He had no real job. He scribbled a bit and said one day he'd be famous.

"I did my best. But I couldn't hold on to him. Sometimes I was away three days on end. . . . It wasn't much fun for him to come back to an empty place and get his own meals. What do you think yourself, Chief Inspector?"

"I don't know."

The man showed surprise. That a senior functionary of the police should have no definite opinion was beyond his understanding.

"Don't you think he's guilty?"

"So far there's nothing to prove it, any more than there's anything to prove the contrary."

"Do you think this woman has been good for him? She didn't even take the trouble to put on a dress when he introduced us; she came in slacks, with shoes that were more like clogs. . . . She hadn't even combed her hair. . . . It's true, one sees others like that in the streets. . . ."

There was a lengthy pause while Monsieur Ricain shot hesitant glances at the Chief Inspector. Finally he pulled a worn wallet from his pocket and took several hundred-franc notes from it.

"It will be best if I don't go and see him myself. If he wants to see me, he knows where I live. . . . I suppose he still has no money. He might need some to get himself a good lawyer. . . ."

A pause. A question.

"Have you any children, Chief Inspector?"

"Unfortunately, no."

"He mustn't feel abandoned. Whatever he's done, if he's done anything wrong, he isn't responsible. . . . Tell him that's what I think. Tell him he can come to the house any time he wants. I don't insist. . . . I understand. . . ."

Moved, Maigret looked at the bank notes that a broad calloused hand with square fingernails was pushing across the desk.

"Well . . ." sighed the father, as he rose, crumpling his hat in his hands. "If I understand you right, I can still hope he's innocent. Mind you, I'm sure of it. . . . The papers can say what they like, I cannot bring myself to believe that he's done such a thing. . . ."

The Chief Inspector accompanied him to the door, shook the hand that was offered hesitantly.

"Can I keep on hoping?"

"One must never despair."

Alone once again, he was on the point of telephoning Doctor Pardon. He would have liked to chat, to put various questions to him. Pardon was no psychiatrist, to be sure, nor was he a professional psychologist.

But in his career as a general practitioner he had seen all kinds, and often his advice had reinforced Maigret in his opinions.

At that time Pardon would be in his

office with a score of patients lined up in the waiting room. Their monthly dinner was not due until the following week.

It was curious: suddenly, for no precise reason, he had a painful sensation of loneliness.

He was no more than a cog in the complicated machinery of justice, and he had at his disposal specialists, inspectors, the telephone, the telegraph, all kinds of desirable services; above him there were the Public Prosecutor, the Magistrate, and, in the last resort, the judges and juries of the Court of Assizes.

Why, at that point, did he feel responsible? It seemed to him that the fate of a human being depended on him, he still did not know which one—the man or woman who had taken the gun from the drawer in the white painted chest and fired it at Sophie.

A detail had struck him, from the outset, that he had not yet managed to explain. It is rare in the course of a dispute, or in a moment of emotion, for a person to aim at the head.

The reflex action, even in self-defense, is to shoot at the chest, and only professionals shoot at the stomach, knowing that victims of stomach wounds rarely recover.

From a distance of about three feet, the murderer had aimed at the head. . . . To make it look like suicide?

He had left the weapon in the studio. At least if Ricain was to be believed. . . .

The couple came home, at about ten o'clock. He needed money. Francis left his wife behind in Rue Saint-Charles, which was unusual for him, while he set off in search of Carus or some other friend who might be able to lend him two thousand francs. . . .

Why wait until that night if the money had to be handed over next morning?

He went back to the Old Wine Press, half opened the door to see whether the producer had arrived. . . .

At that time Carus was already in Frankfurt, a fact they were just cross-checking at Orly. He hadn't mentioned his journey to Bob or any other member of the little group. . . .

Nora, on the other hand, was in Paris. . . . Not in her suite at the Raphael, as she had claimed that morning, since the concierge's register contradicted her story. . . .

Why had she lied? Did Carus know she was absent from the hotel? Hadn't he telephoned her, on arriving at Frankfurt?

The telephone rang.

"Hello. . . . Doctor Delaplanque. . . . Shall I put him through? . . ."

"Please do. . . . Hello!"

"Maigret? Sorry to disturb you, but there's something that's been bothering me since this morning. . . . I didn't mention it in my report because it's rather vague. In the course of the autopsy, I came across faint marks on the wrists of the corpse, as if someone had grasped them with some force. You couldn't call them bruises, properly speaking. . . ."

"I'm listening."

"That's all. . . . While I can't positively say there was a struggle, I wouldn't be surprised if there had been. I picture the aggressor seizing the victim by the wrists and pushing her . . . She might have fallen against the couch, recovered, and it would have been just before she was upright again that the shot was fired. . . . That would explain why the bullet was taken from the wall three feet and ten inches from the floor, whereas if the girl had been standing upright . . ."

"I follow. . . . Are the marks very light?"

"There's one more pronounced than the others. It could be a thumb, but I can't say anything for sure. That's why I can't record

it officially. You may be able to make something of it. . . ."

"The way things are at the moment I'm
ready to try to make something of anything
that's available. Thank you, Doctor."

Janvier was standing, silent, in the door-
way.

He had returned to the neighborhood by
himself this time, with an obstinate expression, as if it were a matter to be settled
between Boulevard de Grenelle and himself.
He had walked along the banks of the
Seine, and paused forty yards upstream from
the Bir-Hakeim bridge, at the spot where
the gun had been thrown in and fished out
of the river, then he set off in the direction
of the big new apartment house in Boulevard de Grenelle.

Eventually he had gone in and rapped
on the glass-fronted porter's lodge. The girl
inside was young and alluring, and she had
a small, well-lighted sitting room.

After showing her his badge he asked:

"Is it your job to collect the rents?"

"Yes, Inspector."

"You know François Ricain, I presume?"

"They live on the courtyard and they seldom pass by here. . . . I mean, seldom *used*

187

to pass by here. . . . But she . . . I knew them, of course, but it wasn't pleasant always having to dun them for money. In January they asked for a month to pay, then on the fifteenth of February they asked for another delay. The landlord had decided to put them out if they hadn't paid the two outstanding amounts by the fifteenth of March. . . ."

"And they didn't?"

"That was the day before yesterday, the fifteenth. . . ."

Wednesday. . . .

"Weren't you concerned when you didn't see them?"

"I didn't expect them to pay. In the morning he didn't come for his mail, and I said to myself he didn't want to face me. Anyway, they didn't get many letters. . . . Mostly prospectuses and magazines he subscribed to. In the afternoon I went and knocked on their door and nobody answered. . . .

"On Thursday I knocked again, and as there still was no answer I asked a tenant whether she had heard anything. It even occurred to me that they might have bolted. It would be easy for them because of the

188

entrance on Rue Saint-Charles, which is always open. . . ."

"What's your opinion of Ricain?"

"I didn't pay much attention to him. . . . Every so often the tenants complained that they had been having a row or had guests in till all hours, but there are others in the building who don't exactly creep about on tiptoe either, especially the young ones. . . . He looked like some sort of artist. . . ."

"And she?"

"What do you expect me to say? They were skating on thin ice. It's not much of a life. . . . Are you sure she didn't kill herself?"

He was learning nothing new, nor really seeking to learn anything. He was prowling, taking in the streets of the neighborhood, the houses, the open windows, the interiors of the shops.

At seven o'clock he pushed open the door of the Old Wine Press and was almost disappointed not to see Fernande perched on her bar stool.

Bob Mandille was reading the evening paper at one of the tables, while the waiter was finishing setting the tables, arranging a glass vase with a rose on each of the checked tablecloths.

"Hello! The Chief Inspector. . . ."

Bob rose and came over to shake hands with Maigret.

"Well? What have you found out? The newspapers aren't too happy. . . . They say you're clamming up and keeping them at arm's length. . . ."

"Simply because we have nothing to tell them."

"Is it true you have released Francis?"

"He was never detained and he is free to come and go. Who's been talking to you about it?"

"Huguet, the photographer, who lives in the same building on the fourth floor. That's the one who's already had two wives, and has given a child to a third. He saw Francis in the courtyard as he was coming back home. I'm surprised he hasn't been in to see me. . . . Tell me, has he got any money?"

"I gave him twenty francs for a bite to eat and a bus fare."

"In that case it won't be long now before he's here. Unless he's called at his newspaper and by a miracle there was some spare cash in the till. It does happen sometimes. . . ."

"You didn't see Nora Wednesday night?"

"No, she didn't come in. Besides, I can't

remember ever seeing her without Carus. He was on a trip. . . ."

"In Germany, yes. She went out alone. I wonder where she could have gone."

"Didn't she say?"

"She claims she went back to the Raphael around nine o'clock."

"Isn't it true?"

"The concierge's register says it was more like eleven."

"Strange. . . ."

Bob's thin, ironical smile made a sort of crack in the fixed mask of his face.

"Does it amuse you?"

"You must admit that Carus would not have let such an opportunity slip! He took advantage of every occasion without any inhibitions. . . . It would be funny if Nora, for her part . . . But somehow I can't believe it of her. . . ."

"Because she's in love with him?"

"No. Because she is too intelligent and too level-headed. She would not risk losing everything, just when she was so near to achieving her objective, for the sake of an adventure, even with the most attractive man in the world."

"Perhaps she wasn't so near to achieving her objective as you think."

"What do you mean?"

"Carus used to meet Sophie regularly in an apartment in Rue François-Premier specially rented for the purpose."

"Was it as serious as that?"

"So he claims. He even says she was star material and that she would soon have become one."

"Are you serious? Carus, who . . . But she was just a mere girl, the kind you find thirteen to the dozen. . . . You've only got to walk down the Champs-Elysées and you can pick up enough like her to cover all the screens in the world. . . ."

"Nora knew about their liaison."

"Well, that beats me. . . . It's true, if I were to believe all I hear every time a customer pours his heart out to me, I would have ulcers. Go and tell my wife about it. She'd be upset if you didn't pop in to pass the time of day. She's got a soft spot for you. . . . How about a drink?"

"Not right now. . . ."

The kitchen was bigger, more modern than he had supposed. As he expected, Rose wiped her hand before offering it to him.

"So, you've decided to let him go?"

"Are you surprised?"

"I really don't know. . . . Everybody who

comes in here has a version of his own. For some, Francis did it out of jealousy. For others, it's a lover she wanted to get rid of. . . . And for others still, a woman was having her revenge. . . ."

"Nora?"

"Who told you that?"

"Carus was having a serious affair with Sophie. Nora knew about it. He was planning to launch her. . . ."

"Is that true, or are you just making it up to get me talking?"

"It's true. Does it surprise you?"

"Me? It's a long time now since I was surprised by anything. If you were in this business like me . . ."

The idea never occurred to her that one acquires a certain experience of human beings in Police Headquarters.

"But if it's Nora who did it you'll have trouble proving it. She's sharp enough to outwit the whole bunch of you. . . .

"Will you be eating here? I've got duck *à l'orange*. . . . As a first course I can offer you two or three dozen scallops just in from La Rochelle. My mother sent them. . . . Ah, yes. . . . She's turned seventy-five and she goes every morning to the market. . . ."

Huguet, the photographer, arrived with

his companion. Huguet was a pink youth with an innocent face and jovial expression, and he looked as if he was proud to be seen with a woman seven months pregnant.

"Do you know each other? Chief Inspector Maigret . . . Jacques Huguet . . . His girl friend. . . ."

"Jocelyne," Huguet put in, as if it were important or as if it gave him pleasure to pronounce this poetic name.

And, with exaggerated attentiveness, almost as though he were making fun of her:

"What's your drink, my darling?"

He smothered her with little attentions, enveloped her with warm and tender glances, as if to say to the others:

"As you can see, I am in love and I am not ashamed. . . . We have made love. . . . We are expecting a child. . . . We are happy. . . . And it makes no difference to us if you find us ridiculous."

"What will you have, my children?"

"A fruit juice for Jocelyne. A port for me. . . ."

"And what about you, Monsieur Maigret?"

"A glass of beer."

"Hasn't Francis come yet?"

"Have you a date with him here?"

194

"No, but it strikes me he would probably like to see his friends again. If only to show them that he's free, and that you couldn't keep him there. . . . He's like that."

"Did you have the impression that we intended to keep him locked up?"

"I don't know. It's difficult to tell what the police are going to do. . . ."

"Do you think he killed his wife?"

"What difference does it make whether it was he or someone else! She's dead, isn't she? If Francis killed her, it's because he had good reasons. . . ."

"What reasons, in your opinion?"

"I don't know. . . . He'd got fed up with her, perhaps? Or else she made scenes? Or perhaps she was deceiving him? One must let people lead the lives they want, mustn't we, my pet?"

Some customers came in, not regulars, and hesitated to go to a table.

"Three?"

It was a middle-aged couple and a young girl.

"This way. . . ."

This was Bob's big moment: the menu, the whispered advice, the praise for the Charentes wine, for the *chaudrée* . . .

Occasionally he addressed a wink to his companions who had remained at the bar.

It was then that Ricain came in, stopped in his tracks on seeing the Chief Inspector with Huguet and the pregnant girl.

"So there you are!" cried the photographer. "Well, what happened? . . . We thought you were in the darkest depths of some prison."

Francis forced a smile.

"As you see, I'm here. Good evening, Jocelyne. Have you come for me, Inspector?"

"Just now, for the duck *à l'orange.* . . ."

"What will you have?" Bob came over to ask after passing on the order to the waiter.

"Is that port?"

He hesitated.

"No . . . a Scotch. Unless I've run out of credit . . ."

"Today I'll give you credit."

"And tomorrow?"

"That depends on the Chief Inspector."

Maigret was a little put out by the tone of the conversation, but he supposed this was a special brand of humor peculiar to the group.

"Did you go to the newspaper?" he asked Ricain.

"Yes. . . . How did you know?"

"Because you needed money. . . ."

"I just managed to get an advance of a hundred francs against what they owe me. . . ."

"And Carus?"

"I didn't call on him."

"But you were looking for him everywhere on Wednesday evening, and nearly all the night as well."

"It's not Wednesday any more. . . ."

"By the way," the photographer put in, "I've seen Carus. I went to the studio and he was giving some girl I don't know a screen test. . . . He even asked me to take some pictures."

Maigret wondered whether he had had some taken of Sophie as well.

"He's dining here. At least, that was his intention at three o'clock this afternoon, but with him you never know. . . . Especially with Nora. . . . By the way, I ran into Nora too."

"Today?"

"Two or three days ago. In a place where I never expected to see her. . . . A small night club in Saint-Germain-des-Prés, where you see nothing but teen-agers. . . ."

"When was this?" asked Maigret, suddenly attentive.

"Wait now. . . . It's Saturday. . . . Friday. . . . Thursday. . . . No, on Thursday I was at the opening of the ballet. It was Wednesday. I was looking for pictures to illustrate an article on teen-agers. I had been told about this club. . . ."

"What time was that?"

"Around ten o'clock. . . . Yes, I must have got there at ten o'clock. . . . Jocelyne was with me. What do you think, sweetie? It was ten o'clock, wasn't it? A crummy place, but picturesque, with all the boys wearing hair down to their collars. . . ."

"Did she see you?"

"I don't think so. She was in a corner, with a beefy character who certainly wasn't a teen-ager. . . . I suspect he was the proprietor, and they looked as if they were talking seriously about something."

"Did she stay long?"

"I fought my way into the two or three rooms where almost everybody was dancing. Well, if you can call that dancing. . . . They were doing their best, glued together. . . .

"I got another glimpse or two of her, between the heads and the shoulders. She was still deep in conversation. The character had taken a pencil from his pocket and was writing figures on a piece of paper. . . .

"It's funny, now that I think about it. . . . As it is, she doesn't look quite real. But there, in that crazy atmosphere, it would have been worth a photograph. . . ."

"Didn't you take one?"

"I'm not such an idiot! I don't want trouble with Papa Carus. I rely on him for a good half of my meal ticket. . . ."

They heard Maigret order:

"Another beer, Bob. . . ."

His voice, his manner, were no longer quite the same.

"Could you reserve the table I had yesterday?"

"Aren't you going to eat with us?" asked the photographer in surprise.

"Another time."

He needed to be alone, to reflect. Once again, by chance, the pieces that he had carefully fitted together had been thoroughly scrambled, and nothing held together any more.

Francis was covertly watching him, with an anxious expression. Bob, too, was aware of the change.

"You look as if you were surprised to

199

learn that Nora would go to a place like that. . . ."

But the Chief Inspector had turned to Huguet:

"What's the club called?"

"Do you want to make a study of beatniks, too? Wait. . . . It's not a very original name. . . . It must date from the time when it was just a *bistrot* for tramps. The Ace of Spades. . . . Yes. On the left as you go up. . . ."

Maigret emptied his glass.

"Keep my corner for me," he repeated.

A few moments later, a taxi was taking him to the other side of the river.

The place, by day, was colorless. There were only three long-haired customers to be seen and a girl in a man's jacket and trousers smoking a small cigar. A character in a cardigan hustled in from the second room and took up his place behind the bar, a suspicious look in his eye.

"What'll it be?"

"A beer," said Maigret mechanically.

"And after that?"

"Nothing."

"No questions?"

"What do you mean?"

"That I wasn't born yesterday, and that

if Chief Inspector Maigret comes here it isn't because he's thirsty. So I'm waiting for the commercial."

Playfully, the man poured himself a short drink.

"Somebody came in to see you on Wednesday evening. . . ."

"Hundreds of somebodies, if you will permit me to correct you."

"I'm referring to a woman, with whom you spent a long time in conversation."

"Half of the people were women and I was in conversation, as you put it, with quite a lot of them."

"Nora."

"Now we're talking. Well . . . ?"

"What was she doing here?"

"What she comes to do here once a month, on the average."

"That is to say . . . ?"

"Look at the books."

"Because . . . ?"

Astounded, Maigret guessed the truth before the man told him.

"Because she's the boss, that's why, Inspector. She doesn't shout about it . . . I'm not even sure Papa Carus is in the picture. Everyone has the right to do what they like with their money, haven't they?

"I haven't said anything, you know. . . . You tell me a story and I don't say yes or no. . . . Even if you ask me if she owns any other night clubs of the same sort . . ."

Maigret looked at him, questioningly, and the man flickered his eyelids affirmatively.

"There are some people who know which way the wind blows," he concluded lightly. "It's not always the ones who think themselves clever who make the best investments. With three clubs like this, for just one year, I'd retire to the Riviera. . . .

"So, with a dozen, and some of them in the Pigalle area and one on the Champs-Elysées . . ."

SEVEN

WHEN Maigret returned to the Old Wine Press, they had placed three tables end to end and started to eat their dinner all together. On seeing him, Carus rose to his feet and came over, checked napkin in hand.

"I trust you will give us the pleasure of joining us?"

"Please don't be offended if I prefer to eat alone in my corner."

"Are you afraid to have dinner with somebody you will be forced to arrest sooner or later?"

He looked him in the eyes.

"There's every chance, isn't there, that poor Sophie's murderer is among us this evening? Well! . . . As you wish. But we shall ask you at least to have a glass of armagnac with us."

Bob had shown him to his table, in the corner by the revolving door, and he had ordered the scallops and *caneton à l'orange* that Rose had recommended.

He could see them side-view, in two rows. It was obvious, from first glance, that Carus was the dominant figure. His manner, his bearing, his gestures, his voice, his look had the self-assurance of a man of importance.

Ricain had taken a place opposite him unwillingly, it seemed, and only joined half-heartedly in the conversation. As for Dramin, he was with a young girl whom Maigret had not yet met, a rather dim creature with scarcely any make-up, soberly dressed, whom Bob later described as a film cutter.

Maki ate a lot, drank his liquor neat, looked at his companions one after another, and replied to their questions with grunts.

It was Huguet, the photographer, who talked back to the producer most of the time. He seemed to be in top form and kept gazing with proprietary satisfaction at the belly of the placid Jocelyne.

It was not possible, from a distance, to follow the conversation. But from odds and ends of phrases, from exclamations and facial expressions, Maigret managed more or less to follow the sense.

"We'll soon see whose turn is next . . ." the facetious photographer had said, or words to that effect.

And his eyes looked for a moment in Maigret's direction.

"He's watching us. He's peeling off our skins. . . . Now that he's got all he can from Francis, he'll turn on someone else. . . . If you go on making such a sour face, Dramin, he'll pick on you. . . ."

Several lone diners, watching from a distance, envied their merriment. Carus had ordered champagne, and there were two bottles cooling in silver buckets. Bob himself went over to pour it.

Ricain was drinking heavily. It was he who was drinking the most, and he did not smile once at the photographer's cracks, not all of which were in the best of taste.

"Look natural, Francis. Don't forget that the eye of God is fastened upon you. . . ."

Maigret was the butt of his humor. Were they funnier on other evenings when they got together?

Carus was doing his best to help Huguet ease the tension. As for Nora, she turned her cold eyes on each of them in turn.

Beneath it all, the dinner was a gloomy affair and nobody was behaving quite naturally, perhaps partly because they were all reacting to the Chief Inspector's presence.

"I bet you'll turn out a script one

day that our good friend Carus will pro-
duce. . . . All tragedies end that way."

"Shut up, will you?"

"I'm sorry. I didn't know you would . . ."

It was worse when they were silent. In
reality there was no friendship between
them. It was not free choice that brought
them together. Each one had an ulterior
motive.

Weren't they all dependent on Carus?
Above all Nora, who extracted from him
the means to buy her night clubs. She had
no guarantee that he would marry her one
day, and she chose to take precautions.

Did he suspect anything? Did he imagine
that he was loved for himself?

It was unlikely. He was a realist. He
needed a companion, and for the time being
she filled the bill well enough. He was probably pleased that her appearance was striking enough to attract attention wherever they
went together.

"That's Carus and his friend Nora. . . .
Isn't she stunning?"

Why not? He had none the less become
Sophie's lover, and was planning to make a
star of her.

This presupposes that he would get rid of

Nora. He had had others before her. He would have others after. . . .

Dramin lived in a world of unfinished scripts to which Carus had the power to give life. So long as he believed in his talent . . .

Francis was in the same boat, with the difference that he was less humble, less patient, that he was readily aggressive, especially when he had had a few drinks. . . .

As for Maki, he kept his thoughts to himself. His sculpture did not sell, yet . . . While he was waiting for the dealers to show some interest, he painted scenery, good or bad, for Carus and anybody else, content when he did not have to pay for his dinner, eating twice as much on such occasions and ordering the most expensive dishes on the menu.

The photographer, now . . . Maigret found it less easy to read his character in his face. At first sight he did not seem to matter. In nearly all groups which get together frequently, one finds this sort of simpleton character, with big, frank eyes, who plays the role of buffoon. His transparent honesty allowed him to put his foot in his mouth, and every now and then to come out with a home truth nobody else would have got away with.

His very job indicated someone of no consequence. . . . They laughed at him and his ever pregnant women.

Rose, wiping her hands, came out to make sure that everybody was satisfied and, without sitting down, accepted a glass of champagne.

Every now and then Bob went and stood beside Maigret.

"They are doing their best," he whispered knowingly.

Sophie was missing. Everyone felt it. How had Sophie behaved on these occasions?

Sulkily, no doubt, or shyly, but with the knowledge, all the same, that she was the one the rich man of the crowd, Carus, favored. In all probability she had met him that same afternoon in the hideaway in Rue François-Premier.

Carus needed them too. It was through launching young people that he made most of his money. To be thus surrounded by a sort of court at the Old Wine Press gave him more of a sense of importance than dining with financiers who were richer and more influential than himself.

A wink to Bob, who brought two fresh

bottles to the big table. Ricain, exasperated by the photographer's gibes, answered him curtly. One could see the moment approaching when, goaded beyond endurance, he would jump to his feet and stalk out. He did not yet dare to do so, but he was straining at the leash.

True, one of them had probably killed Sophie, and Maigret studied their faces, while the heat made the blood rise to his head.

Carus was in Frankfurt on Wednesday evening, of that they had confirmation from Orly. Nora was talking figures between ten and eleven o'clock in the hectic atmosphere of the Ace of Spades.

Maki? . . . But why would Maki want to kill her? . . . He had slept with Sophie, by chance, because she expected it, or so it appeared, of all their friends. It was a way of reassuring herself, of proving she had some charms, that she was not just any other girl caught up in the movies.

Huguet? . . . He already had three women. . . . It seemed to be a mania, like giving them children. It was a wonder he managed to feed all his different broods. . . .

As for Francis . . .

Again Maigret went over Ricain's movements. The return to Rue Saint-Charles, around ten o'clock. . . . The urgent need of money. . . . He had hoped to find Carus at the Old Wine Press, but Carus was not there. . . . Bob had balked at the amount. . . .

He had left Sophie at home. . . .

Why, when he usually took his wife everywhere with him?

"No!" cried the photographer in a loud voice. "Not here, Jocelyne. This is not the time to go to sleep. . . ."

And he explained that since she had been pregnant she had taken to dropping off to sleep, anywhere, any time.

"Some of them crave pickles, some go for pig's feet or calf's head. She sleeps. Not only does she sleep, she snores. . . ."

Maigret attached no importance to the incident, and went on trying to reconstruct Ricain's comings and goings up to the moment when the latter had stolen his wallet, in Rue du Temple, on the platform of the bus.

Ricain, who had not kept a *centime* for himself . . . Ricain, who had telephoned to tell him . . .

He filled his pipe, lit it. Anybody might

have thought that he, too, was dozing off in his corner over his coffee.

"Won't you come and have one for the road with us, Inspector?"

Carus again. Maigret decided to accept, and sit with them for a moment.

"Well," laughed Huguet, "whom are you going to arrest? . . . It's impressive enough to know you're there, watching all our expressions. . . . Every now and then I even begin to feel guilty myself."

Ricain looked so ill that nobody was surprised when he suddenly got to his feet and headed for the lavatory.

"There should be a drinking license, like a driving license," said Maki dreamily.

The sculptor would certainly have got one at the drop of a hat, for he had drained glass after glass and the only effect was to make his eyes shine and his face turn brick red.

"It's always the same with him. . . ."

"Your health, Monsieur Maigret," Carus was saying, holding up his glass. "I was going to say, to the success of your inquiry, since we are all eager for you to find out the truth. . . ."

"All except one!" the photographer corrected him.

"Except one, perhaps. Unless it is not one of us. . . ."

When Francis returned, his eyelids were red and his face had lost its composure. Without being asked, Bob brought a glass of water.

"Do you feel better now?"

"Alcohol doesn't agree with me. . . ."

He was avoiding Maigret's eyes.

"I think I'm going home to bed. . . ."

"Won't you wait for us?"

"You forget I haven't had much sleep these past three days. . . ."

He looked younger, in his physical disarray, much like an overgrown schoolboy ashamed of being made ill by his first cigar.

"Good night. . . ."

They watched Carus get up, follow him over to the door, speak to him in a low voice. Then the producer sat at the table which Maigret had occupied, pushed away the coffee cup, and made out a check while Francis waited, his eyes averted.

"I couldn't leave him in the lurch. If I had been in Paris on Wednesday, perhaps nothing would have happened. I would have had dinner here. He would have asked me for his rent money and he wouldn't have had to leave Sophie. . . ."

Maigret started, turned the phrase over in his mind, looked at each of them in turn.

"If you will excuse me, I will leave you now."

He needed to be out of doors; he was beginning to suffocate. Perhaps he had drunk too much, too? In any case, he did not finish the enormous glass of armagnac.

Without any precise aim, and with his hands in his pockets, he wandered along the sidewalks where several shop windows remained lit. Couples, mainly, were stopping to stare at the washing machines and television sets. Young couples dreaming, making calculations.

"Hundred-franc monthly installments, Louis . . ."

"Plus two hundred and fifty on the car . . ."

Francis and Sophie must have walked like this, arm in arm, in this neighborhood.

Did they dream of washing machine and television set?

They did have a car, the battered old Triumph which Ricain had abandoned somewhere during that fateful Wednesday night. Had he gone back to get it?

With the check he had just received he had enough to pay his rent. . . . Did he

213

intend to live by himself in the studio where his wife had been murdered?

Maigret crossed the boulevard. An old man was sleeping on a bench. The big new building towered in front of him, with about half of its windows lit.

The other tenants were at the movies, or else they were lingering on, as they were at the Old Wine Press, at restaurant tables.

The air remained balmy, but some large clouds would shortly be passing in front of the full moon.

Maigret turned the corner of Rue Saint-Charles and went into the courtyard. Light could be seen in a small window with frosted glass beside Ricain's door, the window of the bathroom with the hip bath.

Other doors, other windows, also lit, both on the studio side and in the main building. . . .

The courtyard was deserted, silent, the trash cans in place, a cat making its way stealthily along the wall. . . .

Now and then a window would shut, and a light would go out. Early bedders. Then, on the fourth floor, a window lit up. It was a little like the stars which suddenly begin to shine brightly or disappear in the sky.

He thought he could make out, behind

the blind, the voluminous silhouette of Jocelyne, and the outline of the photographer's disheveled hair.

Then his eye traveled from the fourth floor to the ground floor.

"At about ten o'clock . . ."

He knew the timetable of that night by heart. The Huguets had dined at the Old Wine Press, and as they had been sitting by themselves the meal must have been brief. What time had they come home?

As for Ricain and Sophie, they had opened the studio door and switched on the lights somewhere near ten o'clock. Then, almost immediately afterwards, Francis had gone out. . . .

Maigret could still see the human shapes, high up, coming and going. Then there was only one, the photographer's. . . . The man opened the window, looked at the sky for a moment. . . . Just as he was about to go off, his eye fell upon the courtyard. He must have seen the lighted studio window and, in the center of the empty space, Maigret's silhouette etched in the moonlight. . . .

The Chief Inspector emptied his pipe against his heel and went into the building. Coming from the courtyard, he did not have to pass in front of the porter's lodge. He went into the elevator, pushed the button for the fourth floor, and a moment later found himself once again in a hallway.

When he knocked on the door, it was as if Huguet had been waiting for him, for he opened at once.

"It's you!" he said with a curious smile. "My wife is getting ready for bed. . . . Will you come in, or would you rather I came out with you?"

"Perhaps it would be better if we went downstairs."

"One moment. . . . I'll tell her and get my cigarettes."

An untidy sitting room was half visible, with the dress Jocelyne had been wearing that evening thrown on an armchair.

"No. . . . No. . . . I promise I'll be back in a moment. . . ."

Then he lowered his voice. She was whispering. The bedroom door remained ajar.

"Are you sure?"

"Don't worry. See you in a moment."

He never wore a hat. He did not take a coat.

"Let's go. . . ."

The elevator was still there. They took it.

"Which side? The street or the courtyard?"

"The courtyard."

They reached it, walked side by side in
the dark. When Huguet raised his head, he
saw his wife looking out of the window, and
signaled her to go back.

There was still light in Ricain's bathroom.
Was his stomach turning over again?

"Have you guessed?" asked the photographer finally, after a cough.

"I'm just wondering."

"It's not a pleasant situation, you know.
Ever since it happened, I've been trying to
be smart. Just now, at dinner, I spent the
most disagreeable night of my life. . . ."

"It was quite obvious."

"Have you got a match?"

Maigret handed him his matches and
began slowly to fill one of the two pipes he
had in his pocket.

EIGHT

"D ID Ricain and his wife have dinner at the Old Wine Press on Wednesday evening?"

"No. . . . The fact is, they only ate there when they happened to be in funds, or when they could find someone to invite them. They went by at about half past eight. Only Francis went in. . . . Often, in the evenings, he only half opened the door. If Carus was there, he would go on in, with Sophie following, and sit at his table. . . ."

"Whom did he speak to, on Wednesday?"

"When I saw him, he only exchanged a couple of words with Bob. He asked: 'Is Carus here?'

"And when he was told no, he left. . . ."

"He didn't try to borrow money?"

"Not then. . . ."

"If he was counting on Carus to invite him to dinner, does it mean they hadn't eaten?"

"They must have gone for a snack to a

self-service place in Avenue de La-Motte-Picquet. They often used to go there."

"Did you and your wife stay long?"

"We left the Old Wine Press at about nine. We strolled for about a quarter of an hour. We went home and Jocelyne undressed immediately. Since she's been pregnant she's always tired. . . ."

"So I heard."

The photographer looked puzzled.

"You talked about it at dinner. It seems she even snores."

"Both my other two did, as well. . . . I think all women snore when they are a few months pregnant. I said that to tease her. . . ."

They were talking in an undertone, in a silence broken only by the sound of cars in Boulevard de Grenelle, on the far side of the building. Rue Saint-Charles, beyond the open gate, was empty; only at long intervals would the silhouette of a man going by come into view, or a girl tripping past on her high heels.

"What did you do?"

"I saw her to bed and went to say good night to my children. . . ."

His first two wives lived in the same

building, one with two children, the other with one.

"Do you do that every night?"

"Nearly every night. Unless I get home too late. . . ."

"Are you welcome?"

"Why not? They have nothing against me. . . . They know me. They know that's the way I am . . ."

"In other words, one day or other you will leave Jocelyne for somebody else?"

"If it comes to the point. . . . You know, for myself, I don't attach any importance to it. I adore children . . . the greatest man in history was Abraham. . . ."

It was hard not to smile, especially when, as now, he was talking sincerely. Beneath the contrived jokes, there really was a core of genuineness.

"I stayed with Nicole for a moment. . . . Nicole, that's the second one. Sometimes we have a little reunion for old times' sake. . . ."

"Does Jocelyne know?"

"It doesn't bother her. If I wasn't made like that, she wouldn't be with me."

"Did you make love?"

"No. I thought about it. . . . The child

started to talk in its sleep and I tiptoed out."

"What time was this?"

"I didn't look at my watch. I went back home. I changed the film in one of my cameras, because I had to take some pictures early the next morning. Then I went to the window and opened it. . . .

"I open it every night, wide at first, to get rid of the cigarette smoke, then halfway, because, winter or summer, I can't sleep all shut in. . . ."

"Next?"

"I smoked a last cigarette. There was a moon, like tonight. . . . I saw a couple crossing the courtyard and I recognized Francis and his wife. They were not holding hands, as they usually did, and they were having a heated conversation."

"Did you hear anything?"

"Just one thing which Sophie said in a piercing voice, which made me think she was in a furious temper."

"Did she often get that way?"

"No. She said: *'Don't play the innocent. . . . You knew perfectly well . . .'*"

"Did he answer?"

"No. He seized her by the arm and dragged her toward the door. . . ."

"You still don't know what time this was?"

"Yes, I do. I heard the church clock strike ten. A light went on in the bathroom window. I lit another cigarette. . . ."

"Were you curious?"

"I just wasn't sleepy, that's all. I poured myself a glass of calvados. . . ."

"Were you in the living room?"

"Yes. The bedroom door was open and I had put out the lights so Jocelyne could sleep. . . ."

"How long did all this take?"

"The time it took me to finish the cigarette I had lit in my first wife's place, then the one I lit by the window. . . . A little over five minutes? Less than ten, anyway. . . ."

"Did you hear anything?"

"No. I saw Francis leave and go quickly toward the gate. He always kept his car in Rue Saint-Charles. . . . After a while the motor coughed, then, a few moments later, it started."

"When did you go down?"

"A quarter of an hour later. . . ."

"Why?"

"I told you. . . . I wasn't sleepy. I wanted a chat."

"Just a chat?"

"Perhaps a bit more. . . ."

"Had you previously had relations with Sophie?"

"You want to know if I had slept with her. . . . Once. Francis was drunk and as there was nothing left in the house he had gone out to fetch a bottle from a *bistrot* that was still open. . . ."

"Was she willing?"

"It seemed perfectly natural to her. . . ."

"And afterwards?"

"Afterwards, nothing. . . . Ricain came back without the bottle—they had refused to sell him one. We put him to bed. . . . The next few days there was no question of anything more happening. . . ."

"Let's get back to Wednesday evening. You went down . . ."

"I went to the door. I knocked. And so as not to scare Sophie, I whispered: 'It's Jacques. . . .' "

"Nobody answered?"

"No. There wasn't a sound inside. . . ."

"Didn't this strike you as odd?"

"I told myself she had had a row with Francis and didn't want to see anybody. I assumed she was in bed, furious, or in tears. . . ."

"Did you go on trying?"

"I knocked two or three times, then I went upstairs again to my place. . . ."

"Did you go back to the window?"

"When I had got into my pajamas, I looked down into the courtyard. . . . It was empty. The light was still on in the Ricains' bathroom. I climbed into bed and went to sleep. . . ."

"Go on. . . ."

"I got up at eight, made myself some coffee while Jocelyne was still sleeping. . . . I opened the window wide, and I noticed that the light was still on in Francis' bathroom. . . ."

"Didn't it strike you as funny?"

"Not really. These things happen. I went to the studio, where I worked until one o'clock, then I had a bite to eat with a friend. I had a date at the Ritz with an American movie star who kept me cooling my heels for an hour, and then hardly gave me enough time to take pictures of him. What with one thing and another, it was four o'clock before I got back. . . ."

"Hadn't your wife gone out?"

"To do her shopping, yes. After breakfast she had gone back to bed. She was asleep."

He was aware of the comic side to this leitmotif.

"Was there still . . ."

"A light on? Yes. . . ."

"Did you go down and knock on the door?"

"No. I telephoned. Nobody answered. Ricain must have gone back, slept, gone out with his wife, forgetting to turn out the light."

"Did that happen sometimes?"

"It happens to everybody. Let's see . . . Jocelyne and I went to a movie in the Champs-Elysées. . . ."

Maigret just managed to stop himself from asking:

"Did she fall asleep?"

The cat came and rubbed itself against his trouser leg and looked at him as if demanding to be stroked. But when Maigret bent down, it moved quickly away and miaowed at him from a few feet farther on.

"Whom does it belong to?"

"I don't know. . . . Everybody. . . . People throw it scraps of meat from the window and it lives outdoors."

"What time did you come back on Thursday evening?"

"Around ten thirty. After the movies we had a drink in a *brasserie* and I met a friend. . . ."

"The light?"

"Of course. But there was nothing surprising about that because the Ricains might well have been back. Even so, I phoned. I admit I was a bit worried when I didn't get an answer. . . ."

"Only a bit?"

"Well, I didn't suspect the truth. If one were to imagine a murder every time somebody forgets to switch off the light . . ."

"In short . . ."

"Look! He hasn't put out his light now, either. I don't think he can be working. . . ."

"Next morning?"

"Of course I telephoned again, and twice more during the day, until I learned from the newspaper that Sophie was dead. I was at Joinville, in the studios, taking stills for a film being made . . ."

"Did someone answer?"

"Yes. A voice I don't know. I decided to say nothing and hung up after waiting a few moments. . . ."

"You didn't try to get hold of Ricain?"

Huguet said nothing. Then he shrugged

his shoulders and resumed his comic expression.

"Look, I don't work at the Quai des Orfèvres!"

Maigret, who was staring idly at the light diffused by the frosted glass, suddenly started toward the studio door. Thinking he understood, the photographer went after him.

"While we were busy chatting . . ."

If Francis wasn't working, if he wasn't sleeping, if the light was still on, that night . . .

He hammered violently on the door.

"Open up! It's Maigret. . . ."

He was making so much noise that a neighbor appeared at his door in pajamas. He looked at the two men in astonishment.

"Now what's going on? Can't one have a moment's peace?"

"Run to the concierge. Ask her if she has a passkey."

"She hasn't."

"How do you know?"

"Because I already asked her, one evening when I had forgotten my key. I had to call a locksmith. . . ."

For a man who made himself out to be simple, Huguet did not lose his head. Wrapping his handkerchief around his fist, he delivered a blow at the frosted glass, which splintered into fragments.

"We must act fast," he panted, as he looked in.

Maigret looked, too. Fully dressed, Ricain was seated in the bath which was too small for him to lie in. Water was flowing from the tap. The bath was overflowing and the water was pink.

"Have you got a strong screwdriver, a jack, anything heavy?"

"In my car. . . . Wait."

The neighbor went off to put on a dressing gown, and he emerged followed by a barrage of questions from his wife. He went out of the main door, and there was the sound of a car trunk being opened.

As the woman herself appeared, Maigret shouted:

"Call a doctor. The nearest one."

"What's going on? Isn't it enough for . . . ?"

She went off, grumbling, while her husband came back with a jack. He was taller, broader, and heavier than the Chief Inspector.

"Let me do it. As long as I don't have to worry about the damage . . ."

The wood resisted at first, then cracked.

228

Another two heaves, one lower, then one higher up, and the door suddenly yielded, while the man had to stop himself from falling in.

The rest was confusion. Other neighbors had heard the noise, and there were soon several of them in the narrow entrance. Maigret had pulled Francis out of the bath and dragged him over to the divan bed. He remembered the drawer in the chest, and its assortment of contents.

He found some string. With the aid of a large blue pencil he improvised a tourniquet. He had scarcely finished it when a young doctor shouldered him aside. He lived in the building, and had hastily pulled on a pair of trousers.

"How long ago?"

"We've just found him. . . ."

"Telephone for an ambulance."

"Is there any chance of . . . ?"

"For God's sake, don't ask questions!"

The ambulance pulled up in the courtyard five minutes later. Maigret climbed in front beside the driver. At the hospital, he had to wait in the corridor while the acting house surgeon performed a blood transfusion.

He was surprised to see Huguet appear.

"Will he pull out of it?"

"They don't know yet."

"Do you think he really meant to commit suicide?"

It was apparent that he had his doubts. So did Maigret. Cornered, Francis had had to make a theatrical gesture.

"Why do you think he would have done a thing like that?"

The Chief Inspector took the question in the wrong sense.

"Because he considered himself too intelligent."

Naturally, the photographer did not understand and stared at him with some bewilderment.

It was not Sophie's death that Maigret had in mind at that precise moment. It was an event much less serious, but perhaps of greater consequence for Ricain's future: the theft of his wallet.

NINE

HE had slept until ten o'clock, but he had not been able to have his breakfast by the open window as he had been promising himself, for there was a downpour of fine rain.

Before going to the bathroom, which had no window, frosted or otherwise, giving onto the courtyard, he telephoned the hospital and had the greatest difficulty in getting through to the doctor on duty.

"Ricain? . . . What is it? . . . An emergency? . . . We had eight emergencies last night, and if I had to remember all their names . . . Good. . . . Blood transfusion. . . . Attempted suicide. . . . Hm! . . . If the artery had been cut he wouldn't be here, or else we'd have laid him out in the basement. . . . He's all right, yes. . . . He has not opened his mouth. . . . No. . . . Not one word. . . . There's a cop outside his door. . . . Obviously you know all about it. . . ."

At eleven o'clock Maigret was in his office. His feet were hurting him once more. He had decided to put his new shoes on again, since he had to break them in sometime.

Seated opposite Lapointe and Janvier, he began automatically to arrange his pipes in order of size, then he chose one, the longest, and filled it carefully.

"As I was saying, he is too intelligent. Sometimes it's as dangerous as being too stupid. An intelligence not applied along with a certain force of character. No matter! I know what I want to say, even if I can't find the words to express it.

"Besides, it isn't my concern. The doctors and psychiatrists will take care of all that.

"I'm almost sure he was an idealist, an idealist incapable of living up to his ideal. Do you see what I mean?"

Not too clearly, perhaps. Maigret had seldom been so prolix and so confused all at once.

"He would have liked, above all, to be exceptional in all things. To succeed very fast, as he was burning with impatience, but all the while remaining pure. . . ."

He was losing heart, his words lagging far behind his thought.

"The best and the worst. He must have hated Carus, because he needed him. That didn't stop him from accepting the dinners the producer stood him, and he didn't think twice about touching him for a loan.

"He was ashamed of himself. He was angry with himself.

"He was not so naïve that he didn't realize that Sophie hadn't turned into the wife he thought he could see in her. But he needed her, too. He even took advantage, it must be conceded, of her affair with Carus.

"He will refuse to admit it. He can't admit it.

"And that's just the reason he shot his wife. They were already quarreling, on Wednesday evening, as they came into the courtyard. What it was about doesn't matter. She must have been exasperated, watching his two-faced game, and probably spat out the truth in his face.

"I wouldn't be surprised if she called him a pimp. Perhaps the drawer was partly open. At any rate, he could not tolerate hearing a truth of that sort being voiced.

"He shot her. Then he stopped in his tracks, frightened by what he had just done, and by the consequences.

"I'm convinced that from this moment

he made up his mind that he would not let himself be convicted, and while he roamed the streets his brain began to work, to concoct a complicated plan.

"So complicated, in fact, that it almost worked.

"He goes back to the Old Wine Press. He asks for Carus. He needs two thousand francs right away, and he knows Bob isn't the man to lend him a sum like that.

"He has thrown the weapon into the Seine, so as to get around the question of fingerprints.

"He shows his face several times at the Zero Club—'Hasn't Carus got here yet?' —He drinks, walks about ceaselessly adding little touches to his plan.

"True, he hasn't enough money to leave the country, but even if he had it wouldn't be of any use to him, because sooner or later he would be extradited.

"He must get back to Rue Saint-Charles, make a pretense of discovering the body, and alert the police.

"And so he thinks of me.

"He's about to pull an act on me that no normal person would even have dreamed of. The details begin to fall into place. His wanderings are starting to pay dividends.

"He watches me, from early morning, at the door of my house. If I don't take the bus, doubtless he has some alternative solution.

"He steals my wallet. He calls me up, plays his part in such a way as to lead suspicion away from himself.

"And that's just it—he overdoes it! He gives me the menu of Sophie's non-existent dinner at the Old Wine Press. He lacks stability, simple common sense. He can invent an extravagant story and make it plausible, but he doesn't think of the simplest and most mundane details."

"Do you think his case will ever get to the courts, Chief?" asked Lapointe.

"That depends on the psychiatrists."

"What would you decide, yourself?"

"The courts."

And, as his two colleagues showed surprise at such a definite reply, so uncharacteristic of what they knew of the Chief Inspector, Maigret observed:

"He would be too unhappy to be thought mad, or even only partially responsible. In the dock, on the other hand, he will be able to play the role of the exceptional being, a sort of hero."

He shrugged, smiled sadly, went over to the window, and gazed at the rain.

A note on the text
Large print edition designed by
Pauline L. Chin.
Composed in 16 pt Plantin
on a Xyvision 300/Linotron 202N
by Marilyn Ann Richards
of G.K. Hall & Co.